THIS BOOK
BELONGS TO

_____

_____

Anonymous

VINTAGE BOOKS
London

1 3 5 7 9 10 8 6 4 2

Vintage
20 Vauxhall Bridge Road,
London SW1V 2SA

Vintage Children's Classics is part of the Penguin Random House group of
companies whose addresses can be found at
global.penguinrandomhouse.com

Penguin
Random House
UK

First published in Great Britain by Eyre Methuen in 1972
This edition published by Vintage in 2018

www.vintage-books.co.uk

A CIP catalogue record for this book is available from the British Library

ISBN 9781784873172

Typeset in 12/16.7 pt Minion by Jouve (UK), Milton Keynes
Printed and bound by Clays Ltd, St Ives plc

Penguin Random House is committed to a sustainable future for our
business, our readers and our planet. This book is made from Forest
Stewardship Council® certified paper.

September 16

Yesterday I remember thinking I was the happiest person in the whole earth, in the whole galaxy, in all of God's creation. Could that only have been yesterday or was it endless light-years ago? I was thinking that the grass had never smelled grassier, the sky had never seemed so high. Now it's all smashed down upon my head and I wish I could just melt into the blaaaa-ness of the universe and cease to exist. Oh, why, why, why can't I? How can I face Sharon and Debbie and the rest of the kids? How can I? By now the word has gotten around the whole school, I know it has! Yesterday I bought this diary because I thought at last I'd have something wonderful and great and worthwhile to say, something so personal that I wouldn't be able to share it with another living person, only myself. Now like everything else in my life, it has become so much nothing.

I really don't understand how Roger could have done this to me when I have loved him for as long as I can remember and I have waited all my life for him to see me. Yesterday when he asked me out I thought I'd literally and completely die with happiness. I really did! And now the whole world is cold and gray and unfeeling and my mother is nagging me to clean up my room. How can she nag me to clean up my room when I feel like dying? Can't I even have the privacy of my own soul?

Diary, you'll have to wait until tomorrow or I'll have to go through the long lecture again about my attitude and my immaturity.

See ya.

September 17

School was a nightmare. I was afraid I'd see Roger every time I turned a corner in the hall, yet I was desperate for fear I wouldn't see him. I kept telling myself, 'Maybe something went wrong and he'll explain.' At lunch I had to tell the girls about his not showing. I pretended I didn't care, but oh, Diary, I do! I care so much I feel that my whole insides have shattered. How is it possible for me to be so miserable and embarrassed and humiliated and beaten and still function, still talk and smile and concentrate? How could Roger have done this to me? I wouldn't intentionally hurt anyone in this whole world. I wouldn't hurt them physically or emotionally, how then can people so consistently do it to me? Even my parents treat me like I'm stupid and inferior and ever short. I guess I'll never measure up to anyone's expectations. I surely don't measure up to what I'd like to be.

September 19

Dad's birthday. Not much.

September 20

It's my birthday. I'm 15. Nothing.

September 25

Dear Diary,

I haven't written for about a week because nothing of interest has happened. The same old dumb teachers teaching the same old dumb subjects in the same old dumb school. I seem to be kind of losing interest in everything. At first I thought high school would be fun but it's just dull. Everything's dull. Maybe it's just because I'm growing up and life is becoming more blasé. Julie Brown had a party but I didn't go. I've put on seven ugly, fat, sloppy, slobby pounds and I don't have anything I can wear. I'm beginning to look as slobby as I feel.

September 30

Wonderful news, Diary! We're moving. Daddy has been invited to become the Dean of Political Science at ———. Isn't that exciting! Maybe it will be like it was when I was younger. Maybe again he'll teach in Europe every summer and we'll go with him like we used to. Oh those were the fun, fun times! I'm going to start on a diet this very day. I will be a positively different person by the time we get to our new home. Not one more bite of chocolate or nary a french fried potato will pass my lips till I've lost ten globby pounds of lumpy lard. And I'm going to make a completely new wardrobe. Who cares about Ridiculous Roger? Confidentially, Diary, I still care. I guess I'll always love him, but maybe just before we leave and I'm thin and my skin is absolutely flawless and petal smooth and clear, and I have clothes like a fashion model he'll ask me for another date. Shall I turn him down or stand him up or will I – I'm afraid I will – weaken and go out with him?

Oh please, Diary, help me to be strong and consistent. Help me to exercise every morning and night and clean my skin and eat right and be optimistic and agreeable and positive and cheerful. I want so much to be someone important, or even just asked out by a boy every once in a while. Maybe the new me will be different.

October 10

Dear Diary,

I've lost three pounds and we're busy getting sort of semi-organized to move. Our house is up for sale, and Mom and Dad have gone to look for a place in ————. I'm staying here with Tim and Alexandria, and as much as you'll be surprised, they don't even bug me. We're all excited about moving and they do whatever I tell them about helping with the house and meals and such – well, almost. I guess Dad will be taking over the new position at mid-term. He's as excited as a little boy and it's kind of like old times. We sit around the table and laugh and joke and make plans together. It's great! Tim and Alex insist they have to take all their toys and junk. Personally I'd like to get a whole new everything, except my books of course, they are part of my life. When I was hit by a car in the fifth grade and was in a cast for such along time, I'd have died without them. Even now I'm not really sure which parts of myself are real and which parts are things I've gotten from books. But anyway it's great! Life is positively great and wonderful and exciting, and I can't wait to see what's behind the next corner and all the corners after that.

October 16

Mom and Dad came back today. Hooray, we have a house! It's a large old Spanish-type house which Mom loves. I can't wait to move! I can't wait! I can't wait! They took pictures which will be back in three or four days. I can't wait, I can't wait, or have I said that a million times before?

October 17

Even school is exciting again. I got an A on my algebra paper and everything else is going A and B too.

Algebra is the worst. If I can pass that I guess I can do anything! Usually I'm lucky to get a C, even when I kill myself. Isn't it funny, but it seems that when something is going good, everything else goes good too. I'm even getting along better with Mom. She doesn't seem to nag at me so much anymore. I can't figure out which one of us has changed – I really can't. Am I being more whatever it is she wants me to be so she doesn't have to always be on my back or is it she is less demanding?

I even saw Roger in the hall and couldn't have cared less. He said 'hi' to me and stopped to talk, but I just walked on by. He's not going to drop me on my head again! Gee, only a little over three months!

October 22

Scott Lossee asked me to go to the movies Friday. I've lost ten pounds. I'm down to a hundred and fifteen which is all right, but I'd still like to lose another ten pounds. Mom says I don't want to get that thin, but she doesn't know! I do! I do! I do! I haven't had one goodie for so long I've almost forgotten what they taste like. Maybe Friday night I'll go on a binge and eat a few french fries . . . ummmmmmm . . .

The movie was fun with Scott. We went out after and I ate six wonderful, delicious, mouth-watering, delectable, heavenly french fries. That was really living in itself! I don't feel about Scott like I used to about Roger. I guess that was my one and only true love, but I'm glad it's over. Imagine me in my first year of high school and barely fifteen and the one and only great love of my life is over. It seems kind of tragic in a way. Maybe someday when we're both in college we'll meet again. I hope so. I really do hope so. Last summer at Marion Hill's slumber party someone brought in a *Playboy* magazine with a story in it about a girl sleeping with a boy for the first time and all I could think about was Roger. I don't ever want to have sex with any other boy in the whole world ever . . . ever . . . I swear I'll die a virgin if Roger and I don't get together. I couldn't stand to ever have any other boy even touch me. I'm not even sure about Roger. Maybe later when I'm older I'll feel differently. Mother says that as girls get older, hormones invade our bloodstream making our sexual desires greater. I guess I'm just developing slowly. I've heard some pretty wild stories about some of the kids at school, but I'm not them, I'm me, and besides, sex seems so strange and so inconvenient, and so awkward.

I keep thinking about our teacher in gym teaching us modern dance and always saying that it will make our bodies strong and healthy for childbearing, then she harps and harps that everything must be graceful, graceful, graceful. I can hardly picture sex or having a baby as being graceful.

Gotta go. See ya.

November 10

Oh dear Diary, I'm so sorry I've neglected you, but I've been so busy. Here we are preparing for Thanksgiving already and then Christmas. We sold our house last week to the Dulburrows and their seven kids. I do wish we could have sold it to someone with a smaller family. I hate to think of those six boys running up and down our beautiful front stairs with their dirty, sticky fingers on the walls and their dirty feet all over Mother's white carpeting. You know, when I think about things like that, I suddenly don't want to leave! I'm afraid! I've lived in this room all my fifteen years, all my 5,530 days. I've laughed and cried and moaned and muttered in this room. I've loved people and things and hated them. It's been a big part of my life, of me. Will we ever be the same when we're closed in by other walls? Will we think other thoughts and have different emotions? Oh, Mother, Daddy, maybe we're making a mistake, maybe we'll be leaving too much of ourselves behind!

Dear precious Diary, I am baptizing you with my tears. I know we have to leave and that one day I will even have to leave my father and mother's home and go into a home of my own. But ever I will take you with me.

November 30

Dear Diary,

Sorry I didn't talk with you on Thanksgiving. It was so nice, Gran and Gramps were here for two days and we talked about old times and lay around the living room. Daddy didn't even go to his office the whole time. Grandma made taffy with us like she used to when we were little, and even Daddy pulled some. We all laughed a lot, and Alex got it in her hair and Gramps got his false teeth stuck together, and we were almost hysterical. They are sorry we are moving so far away from them and so are we. Home just won't be the same without Gran and Gramps dropping in. I really hope Daddy is right in making the move.

December 4

Dear Diary,

Mama won't let me diet anymore. Just between us, I don't really know why it's any of her business. It's true I have had a cold for the last couple of weeks, but I know it's not the diet that is causing it. How can she be so stupid and irrational? This morning I was having my usual half grapefruit for breakfast and she made me eat a slice of whole wheat bread and a scrambled egg and a piece of bacon. That's probably at least 400 calories, maybe even five or six or seven hundred. I don't know why she can't let me live my own life. She doesn't like it when I look like a cow, neither does anybody else, I don't even like myself. I wonder if I could go stick my finger down my throat and throw up after every meal? She says I'm going to have to start eating dinner again too, and just when I'm getting down where I want to be and I've quit fighting the hunger pangs. Oh, parents are a problem! That's one thing, Diary, you don't have to worry about, only me. And I guess you're not very lucky at that, because I'm certainly no bargain.

December 10

When I bought you, Diary, I was going to write reli-
giously in you every day, but some days nothing worth
writing happens and other days I'm too busy or too
bored or too angry or too annoyed, or just too me to do
anything I don't have to do. I guess I'm a pretty lousy
friend – even to you. Anyway I feel closer to you than I
do to even Debbie and Marie and Sharon who are my
very best friends. Even with them I'm not really me. I'm
partly somebody else trying to fit in and say the right
things and do the right thing and be in the right place
and wear what everybody else is wearing. Sometimes I
think we're all trying to be shadows of each other, trying to buy the same records and everything even if we
don't like them. Kids are like robots, off an assembly
line, and I don't want to be a robot!

December 14

I just bought the most wonderful little single pearl pin
for Mother's Christmas present. It cost me nine dollars
and fifty cents, but it's worth it. It's a cultured pearl
which means it's real and it looks like my Mom. Soft
and shiny, but sturdy and dependable underneath so it

won't dribble all over the place. Oh I hope she likes it! I want so very much for her to like it and for her to like me! I still don't know what I'll get for Tim and Dad, but they're easier to buy for. I'd like to get a nice gold pencil holder or something for Dad to put on his big new desk in his big new office so he'd think of me every time he looked at it, even in the middle of tremendously important conferences with all the leading brains in the world, but as usual I can't afford a fraction of the things I want.

December 17

Lucy Martin is having a Christmas party, and I'm supposed to bring a gelatin salad. It sounds like a lot of fun. (At least I hope it will be.) I've made myself a new white soft wool dress. Mother helped me and it's really beautiful. Someday I hope I can sew as well as she does. In fact someday I hope I can be like her. I wonder if when she was my age she worried about boys not liking her and girls being only her part-time friends. I wonder if boys were as oversexed in those days as they are now? It seems like when we girls talk about our dates that most of the boys are that way. None of my friends ever go all the way, but I guess a lot of the girls at school do. I wish

I could talk to my mother about things like this because I don't really believe a lot of the kids know what they're talking about, at least I can't believe all the stuff they tell me.

December 22

The party at the Martins was fun. Dick Hill brought me home. He had his father's car and we drove all over town and looked at the lights and sang Christmas carols. It sounds kind of corny, but it really wasn't. When we got home he kissed me goodnight, but that's all. It kind of made me nervous because I don't know if he doesn't like me or just respects me or what? I guess I just can't be secure no matter what happens. I sometimes wish I were going with someone then I'd always know I had a date and I'd have someone I could really talk to, but my parents don't believe in that, and besides, confidentially, no one has ever been that interested in me. Sometimes I think no one ever will be. I really do like boys a lot, sometimes I think I like them too much, but I'm not very popular. I wish I were popular and beautiful and wealthy and talented. Wouldn't it be nice to be like that?

December 25

It's Christmas! Wonderful, magnificent, happy, holy Christmas. I'm so happy I can hardly contain myself. I got some books and records and a skirt I really love and a lot of little things. And Mother really loved her pin. She really did! She loved it! She put it right on her nightgown and wore it all day. Oh, I'm so happy she liked it. Gran and Gramps were here and Uncle Arthur and Aunt Jeannie and their kids. It was really great. I guess Christmas is the very best time of the year. Everybody feels warm and secure and needed and wanted. (Even me.) I wish it could be like this all the time. I hated for today to come to an end. Not only because it was such a great day, but because this will be our last big holiday in this lovely house.

Goodbye dear house dressed in your holiday finery of tinsel and holly and bright-colored lights. I love you! I'll miss you!

January 1

Last night I went to a New Year's party at Scott's house. The kids got a little wild. Some of the boys were juicing it up. I came home early saying I didn't feel well, but actually it's just that I'm so excited about moving in two days that I am beside myself. I'm sure I won't sleep at all for the next two nights. Imagine moving into a new home and a new town and a new county and a new state all at the same time. Mom and Dad know a few people on the faculty and they're at least casually acquainted with our new house. I've seen pictures of it, but it still seems like a large, cold, foreboding stranger. I do hope we like it and it can adjust to us.

Frankly, I wouldn't dare say this to anybody but you, Diary, but I'm not too sure I'm going to make it in a new town. I barely made it in our old town where I knew everybody and they knew me. I've never even allowed myself to think about it before, but I really haven't much to offer in a new situation. Oh dear God, help me adjust, help me be accepted, help me belong, don't let me be a social outcast and a drag on my family. Here I go bawling again, what a boob, but there isn't any more I can do about that than there is I can do about moving. So you're wet again! It's a good thing diaries don't catch cold!

January 4

We're here! It's barely January 4, only ten minutes after one, and Tim and Alex have been quarreling and Mama has either the stomach flu or she's just upset because of the excitement; anyway Dad has had to stop twice so that she could throw up. Something went wrong and the lights haven't been turned on and I think even Dad is about ready to turn around and go back home. Mom had made a diagram of where she wanted the movers to put everything and they got it all fouled up. So we're all just going to roll up in bedding and sleep in whichever bed is handy. I'm glad I've got my little pocket flashlight, at least I can see to write. Confidentially the house looks pretty weird and haunted, but maybe that's because there are no curtains up or anything. Maybe things will look brighter tomorrow. They certainly couldn't look worse.

January 6

Sorry I haven't had time to write for two days, but we haven't stopped. We're still trying to get curtains hung and boxes unpacked and things put away. The house is beautiful. The walls are thick dark wood and there are two steps going down to a long sunken living room. I've apologized to every room about the way I felt last night.

I'm still worried about school and TODAY I must go. I wish Tim were in high school. Even a little brother would be better than no one, but he is in his second year of junior high. Already he's met a boy down the street his own age and I should be happy for him, but I'm not – I'm sad for myself. Alexandria is still in grade school and one of the professors lives close and has a daughter her age, so she will go directly to his home after school. How lucky can you get, built-in friends and everything? For me, as usual, nothing! A big fat nothing, and probably just what I deserve. I wonder if the kids wear the same things they do at home? Oh, I hope I'm not so different they'll all stare at me. Oh, how I wish I had a friend! But I better paste on the big phony smile, Mother is calling and I must respond with an 'attitude that will determine my altitude.'

One, two, three, and here goes the martyr.

Evening, January 6

Oh Diary it was miserable! It was the loneliest, coldest place in the world. Not one single person spoke to me during the whole endlessly long day. During lunch period I fled to the nurse's office and said I had a head-ache. Then I cut my last class and went by the drugstore and had a chocolate malt, a double order of french fried potatoes and a giant Hershey Bar. There had to be something in life that was worthwhile. All the time I ate, I hated myself for being childish. Hurt as I am when I think about it I have probably done the same thing to every new person that came to my schools, either ignored them completely or stared at them out of curiosity. So, I'm just getting 'cut' back and I guess I deserve it, but oh, am I ever suffering! I ache even in my fingernails and toenails and in my hair follicles.

January 7

Last night's dinner was excruciating. Alex loves her new school and her new little friend Tricia. Tim rode the bus with the neighbor boy and was in three of his classes, he said the girls were cuter than the ones at his old school and he said they fell all over him, but that's the way it always is when a new boy moves in. Mom went to a tea and found everyone 'charming, beautiful and pleasant.' (Isn't that nice.) Well, like oil and water, I can't quite adapt or fit. Every so often I even seem to be on the outside just looking in on my own family. How can I possibly be such a dud when I come from this gregarious, friendly, elastic background? Gramps was in politics and he was always the favored candidate, with Gran traveling by his side. So what is it with me? Am I some kind of a throwback? A misfit? A mistake!

January 14

A whole week has gone by and no one has done more than stare at me in a kind of curious, hostile, 'what are you doing here?' kind of way. I've tried to bury myself in books and my studies and my music and pretend I don't care. I guess I don't really care, and besides what difference could it possibly make if I did? I've gained five pounds and I don't care about that either. Mother is worried about me I know, because I've become so quiet, but what is there to talk about? If I went by her standing rule of 'If you can't say something nice about things don't say anything at all,' I'd never even open my mouth except to eat, and I've been doing plenty of that!

February 8

Well, I've gained almost fifteen pounds since we've been here, my face is a mess and my hair is so stringy and oily I'd have to wash it every night to keep it decent. Dad is never home and Mom is on my back all the time, 'Be happy, put up your hair, be positive, smile, show some spirit, be friendly,' and if they tell me I'm acting negatively and immaturely one more time I'm going to gag. I can't wear any of the clothes I made before I came here and I know Tim is ashamed of me. When I'm around his friends he treats me like a dum-dum, insults me and makes remarks about my hippy hair. I'm getting fed up to here with this town and school in general and my family and myself in particular.

March 18

Well, I've finally found a friend at school. She's as cloddy and misfitting as I am. But I guess that old poke about birds of a feather is true. One night Gerta came to pick me up for the movies and my folks were everything but rude to her. Imagine my long-suffering, sweet-mouthed mother being tempted to utter a slimy phrase about my drab-looking nobody friend. I wonder why she doesn't take a second look at her drab-looking nobody daughter, or would that be too much for the well-groomed, thin, charming wife of the great Professor, who might be the President of the school within a few years.

I could see them all squirming a little even as I have been squirming ever since we got to this impregnable hole.

April 10

Oh, happiness and joy and elation, Mother has promised me that I can spend the summer at Gran's. I start
on a diet as of today, this very minute! Of course she
had one little string attached to it, as she always does –
that I get my grades back up.

April 20

School is almost over, two more months and I can
hardly wait. Tim is intolerable, and Mother is constantly, constantly picking at me, 'Don't do this – don't
do that – do do this – do do that – why don't you? – you
know you should – now you're acting childish and
immature again.' I know she is always comparing me
with Tim and Alexandria and I just simply can't measure up. It seems like every family has to have one goon,
guess who's *it* on this homestead? It's natural to have a
little sibling rivalry, but ours is getting way out of control. I really do love Tim and Alex, but they've got plenty
of faults too, and I find it difficult to decide whether I
love them more than I hate them or whether I hate them
more than I love them. This also applies to Mom and

Dad! But truthfully I guess it applies even more to myself.

May 5

Every single teacher I have this term is an idiot and a drag. I read once that a person is lucky to have two good teachers who stimulate and motivate him in his whole lifetime. I guess I must have had my two in kindergarten and first grade, right?

May 13

I met another girl walking home from school. She lives just three blocks from us and her name is Beth Baum. She's really awfully nice. She's kind of shy too and prefers books to people just as I do. Her father is a doctor and away from home most of the time just like Dad, and her mother nags a lot but then I guess all mothers do. If they didn't I'd hate to see what homes and yards and even the world would look like. Oh, I do hope I won't have to be a nagging mother, but I guess I'll have to be, else I don't see how anything will ever be accomplished.

May 19

Today I went home with Beth after school. They have a lovely house and a full-time, live-in maid. Beth is Jewish. I've never really had a Jewish friend before, and for some reason I thought they'd be different. I don't know how, because we're all people, but I just thought they'd be . . . well, more like . . . as usual I don't even know what I'm talking about.

Beth is really conscientious and worries about her grades so we did some work and then listened to records and drank no-calorie cokes. (She's trying to lose weight, too.) I really like her and it's nice to have a true friend, for confidentially I didn't really ever feel secure with Gerta, I always wanted to correct her grammar and tell her to watch her clothes and her posture. I guess I'm more like Mom than I thought! It's not that I'm a snob – really it's not. But real friendship can't be built on sympathy and a hanging-on to someone just to keep from drowning. It has to be built on mutual likes and abilities and, yes, even backgrounds. Boy, Mom would be proud of my thinking and attitude today. It's just too bad we can't communicate anymore. I remember being able to talk to her when I was little but it's as though we speak a different language now and the meanings just don't come across the right way. She means something and I take it another way or she says something and I think she's trying to correct me or 'uplift' me or preach at me and I really suspect she isn't doing that at all, just groping and being as lost with words as am I. That's life, I guess.

May 22

Beth came over to my house to study today, and Mom and Dad and both the kids like her! They even asked her to call and get permission to stay for dinner, and then Mom is going to take us downtown shopping since it's Thursday night and the stores are all open. I ran in to change clothes, and Beth ran over to grab her things. We'll pick her up on the way, but I just had to stop and jot the whole ecstatic experience down. It's just too tremendous and delightful and wonderful to keep all bottled-up inside.

May 24

Beth is a wonderful friend. I guess she's the only 'best' friend I've had since I was a very little girl. We can talk about anything. We even talk a lot about religion. The

Jewish Hebrew faith is a lot different than ours. They have their meetings on Saturday and they are still looking for Christ or the Messiah to come. Beth loves her grandparents a lot and she wants me to meet them. She says they are Orthodox and eat meat off one set of plates and milk things off another set of plates. I wish I knew more about my own religion so I could tell Beth.

June 3

Today Beth and I talked about sex. Her grandmother told her that when a Jewish boy and girl are getting married, if someone says the girl isn't a virgin and they can prove it, the boy doesn't even have to marry her. We wondered exactly how they proved such a thing but neither one of us really know. She said she'd rather ask her grandmother than her mother, but I'd rather ask my mother if I were to ask anyone, which of course I won't! And my mother wouldn't know about Jewish customs anyway.

Beth says she has nightmares about walking down the aisle, wearing a long beautiful white gown, with hundreds of people at her wedding and someone whispering to the Rabbi that she's not a virgin and the boy turning around and leaving her. I don't blame her – I'd feel the very same way. Someday when she gets up enough nerve she's going to ask her grandmother or somebody about it. I hope she'll tell me because I really want to know too.

June 10

Dear Diary,

School will soon be over and now I don't want it to end. Beth and I are having such a good time. Neither one of us are very popular with the boys, but sometimes Beth has to go out with the Jewish sons of her mother's friends. She says it's usually a big bore, and the boys don't like her any more than she likes them, but Jewish families are like that, they want their kids to marry other Jewish kids. Some night Beth is going to fix me up on a blind date with 'a nice Jewish boy' to quote her mother. Beth says he'll love it because I'm not Jewish and he'll feel he's putting something over on his mother. I think I like him already.

June 13

Hurrah! School is out! But I'm kind of sad too.

June 15

Beth fixed me up with a boy named Sammy Green. He was incredibly proper and polite to my parents which made them like him, but once we were out in the car he was all hands. Parents really are a poor judge of character. Sometimes I wonder how they made it to the age they are. Anyway the whole night was really stupid. Sam wouldn't even let me watch the movie in peace. Besides it turned out to be such a dirty film that Beth and I stayed in the ladies' room for a long time after it was over. We were both too self-conscious to come out, but since we couldn't spend the night in there, we finally made our grand entrance into the lobby pretending that nothing had ever even happened. The boys tried to discuss the movie, but we both ignored them, and it too.

June 18

Today I received the ghastly news that Beth is going to have to go to summer camp for six weeks. Her folks are going to Europe so they've made arrangements for her at an all-Jewish camp. I am heartbroken and so is she. We've both talked to our parents, but we might as well be talking to the wind. They don't hear us, they don't even listen to us. I guess I'll go spend the summer with Gran as I planned, but even that doesn't seem to hold much interest anymore.

June 23

Beth and I have only two more days together. Our parting is almost like looking forward to a death. It seems that I have known her always for she understands me. I must admit that there were even times when her mother arranged dates for her that I was jealous of the boys. I hope it's not strange for a girl to feel that way about another girl. Oh I hope not! Is it possible that I am in love with her? Oh, that's dumb even for me. It's just that she is the dearest friend that I have ever had or that I shall ever have.

June 25

It is over! At noon Beth is leaving. Last night we said our goodbyes and we both cried and clung to each other like frightened children. Beth is as alone as am I. Her mother is a screamer and tells her she's being childish and silly. At least Mom and Dad are sympathetic and understand how lonely I'm going to be. In fact, Mother took me shopping and let me spend five dollars on a little solid gold necklace with a personal inscription engraved inside, and Dad has told me I can make two long-distance calls to her. That's really pretty decent and thoughtful of them. I guess I am lucky.

July 2

Dear Diary,

I'm at Gran's and I have never been more bored in my life. Talk about a long hot summer – and it isn't even really summer yet! I think I shall lose my mind! I've been reading a book a day since I got here and already I'm bored out of my skull. It's amazing, because during school I really longed for the time to stay in bed and just loaf, loaf, loaf and read, read, read and watch Tely and do the things I want to do, but now I've run out of things. Oh, sheer agony. Sharon has moved and Debbie is going with some guy and Marie is on vacation with her folks. I've only been here five days. I'll have to force myself to at least stay a week before I ask to go home. Can I stand it without going mad?

July 7

Today a very strange thing happened, at least I hope it's going to happen. Oh I do! I do! I do! Gramps and I walked downtown to get a present for Alex's birthday and while we were in the department store, Jill Peters came by. She said 'hi,' and we stopped to talk. I hadn't seen her since we moved away, and I'd never really belonged in her crowd which were kind of the top echelon, but anyway she said she wants to go to Dad's university when she graduates from high school and said she couldn't wait to get out of this little hick town and move to where things really happen. I tried to pretend we were very sophisticated and gay there, but actually I haven't really seen much difference between the two places. I guess I lied a pretty good story though, because she said she was going to have a few kids in tomorrow night and she'd call me. Oh, I do hope she does!

July 8

Oh Diary, I'm so happy I could cry! It did happen! Jill called at exactly 10:32. I know because I'd been sitting by the phone with my watch in my hand trying to send

ESP signals to her. She's having a few kids over for an autograph party, thank heavens I brought my yearbook. It won't be the same as theirs and none of their pictures will be in it, but then mine won't be in theirs either. I'm going to wear my new white pants suit, and I have to go now and wash my hair and put it up. It's really getting long, long, long, but if I put it up on orange juice cans I can make it have just the right amount of body and a nice large curl on the bottom. I hope we have enough cans – we've got to! We've simply got to!

July 10

Dear Diary,

I don't know whether I should be ashamed or elated. I only know that last night I had the most incredible experience of my life. It sounds morbid when I put it in words, but actually it was tremendous and wonderful and miraculous.

The kids at Jill's were so friendly and relaxed and at ease that I immediately felt at home with them. They accepted me like I had always been one of their crowd and everyone seemed happy and unhurried. I loved the atmosphere. It was great, great, great. Anyway, a little while after we got there Jill and one of the boys brought

32

out a tray of coke and all the kids immediately sprawled out on the floor on cushions or curled up together on the sofa and chairs.

Jill winked at me and said, 'Tonight we're playing "Button, Button, Who's Got the Button?" You know, the game we used to play when we were kids.' Bill Thompson, who was stretched out next to me, laughed, 'Only it's just too bad that now somebody has to baby-sit.'

I looked up at him and smiled. I didn't want to appear too stupid.

Everyone sipped their drinks slowly, and everyone seemed to be watching everyone else. I kept my eyes on Jill supposing that anything she did I should do.

Suddenly I began to feel something strange inside myself like a storm. I remember that two or three records had played since we had had the drinks, and now everyone was beginning to look at me. The palms of my hands were sweating and I could feel droplets of moisture on my scalp at the back of my neck. The room seemed unusually quiet, and as Jill got up to close the window shades completely I thought, 'They're trying to poison me! Why, why would they try to poison me?'

My whole body was tense at every muscle and a feeling of weird apprehension swept over me, strangled me, suffocated me. When I opened my eyes, I realized that it was just Bill who had put his arm around my shoulder. 'Lucky you,' he was saying in a slow motioned record on the wrong speed voice, 'But don't worry, I'll baby-sit you. This will be a good trip. Come on, relax, enjoy it, enjoy it.' He caressed my face and neck tenderly, and said, 'Honestly, I won't let anything bad happen to you.' Suddenly he seemed to be repeating himself over and over like a slow-motioned echo chamber. I started laughing, wildly, hysterically. It struck me as the funniest, most absurd thing I had ever heard. Then I noticed the strange shifting patterns on the ceiling. Bill pulled me down and my head rested in his lap as I watched the pattern change to swirling colors, great fields of reds, blues and yellows. I tried to share the beauty with the others, but my words came out soggy, wet and dripping or tasting of color. I pulled myself up and began walking, feeling a slight chill which crept inside as well as outside my body. I wanted to tell Bill, but all I could do was laugh.

Soon whole trains of thought started to appear between each word. I had found the perfect and true and original language, used by Adam and Eve, but when I tried to explain, the words I used had little to do with my thinking. I was losing it, it was slipping out of my grasp, this wonderful and priceless and true thing which must be saved for posterity. I felt terrible, and finally I couldn't talk at all and slumped back onto the floor, closed my eyes and the music began to absorb me physically. I could smell it and touch it and feel it as well as hear it. Never had anything ever been so beautiful. I was a part of every single instrument, literally a part. Each note had a character, shape and color all its very own and seemed to be entirely separate from the rest of the score so that I could consider its relationship to the whole composition, before the next note sounded. My mind possessed the wisdoms of the ages, and there were no words adequate to describe them.

I looked at a magazine on the table, and I could see it in 100 dimensions. It was so beautiful I could not stand the sight of it and closed my eyes. Immediately I was floating into another sphere, another world, another state. Things rushed away from me and at me, taking my breath away like a drop in a fast elevator. I couldn't tell what was real and what was unreal. Was I the table or the book or the music, or was I part of all of them, but it didn't really matter, for whatever I was, I was wonderful. For the first time that I could remember in my whole life, I was completely uninhibited. I was dancing before the whole group, performing, showing off, and enjoying every second of it.

My senses were so up that I could hear someone breathing in the house next door and I could smell someone miles away making orange and red and green ribbed Jell-o.

After what seemed eternities I began to come down and the party started breaking up. I sort of asked Jill what happened and she said that 10 out of the 14 bottles of coke had LSD in them and, 'button, button,' no one knew just who would wind up with them. Wow, am I glad I was one of the lucky ones.

Gramps' house was dark when we got home, and Jill helped me to my room, out of my clothes and into bed, and I drifted off into a seasick type of sleep, wrapped in a general sense of well-being, except for a slight headache that probably was the result of long and intense laughing. It was fun! It was ecstatic! But I don't think I'll ever try it again. I've heard too many frightening stories about drugs.

Now that I think back I should have known what was happening! Any dum-dum should have known, but I thought the whole party was so strange and exciting that I guess I just wasn't listening or maybe I didn't want to listen – I'd have been scared to death if I'd known. So I'm glad they did it to me, because now I can feel free and honest and virtuous about not having made the decision myself. And besides the whole experience is over and past and I'll never think of it again.

Dear Diary,

For two days now I've tried to convince myself that using LSD makes me a 'dope addict' and all the other low-class, unclean, despicable things I've heard about kids that use LSD and all the other drugs; but I'm so, so, so, so, so curious, I simply can't wait to try pot, only once, I promise! I simply have to see if it's everything that it's cracked up not to be! All the things I've heard about LSD were obviously written by uninformed, ignorant people like my parents who obviously don't know what they're talking about; maybe pot is the same. Anyway Jill called this morning, and she's going to her friend's for the weekend and she'll call me the first thing Monday.

I told her what a great, great, great time I had and she seemed pleased. I'm sure if I hint around she'll see that I get to try pot just once, then I'll immediately go home and forget the whole drug set-up, but it's nice to be informed and know what things are really like. Of course, I wouldn't want anyone to know I've really used them, and I guess I better go get one of those little fishing tackle-type metal boxes to lock you in with a good padlock. I can't take a chance on anyone reading you, especially not now! In fact, I guess I better take you with me even to the library to look up something about drugs. Thank goodness for the catalogue section, I wouldn't dare ask anyone. Also if I go now when the library first opens I'll probably have the whole place to myself.

July 14

On the way to the library I met Bill. He's taking me out tonight. I can't wait to see what happens. It's a completely new world I'm exploring, and you can't even conceive the wide new doors that are opening up before me. I feel like Alice in Wonderland. Maybe Lewis G. Carroll was on drugs too.

July 20

Dear close, warm, intimate friend, Diary,

What a fantastic, unbelievable, expanding, thrilling week I've had. It's been like, wow – the greatest thing that has ever happened. Remember I told you I had a date with Bill? Well he introduced me to torpedos on Friday and Speed on Sunday. They are both like riding shooting stars through the Milky Way, only a million, trillion times better. The Speed was a little scary at first because Bill had to inject it right into my arm. I remembered how much I hated shots when I was in the hospital, but this is different, now I can't wait, I positively can't wait to try it again. No wonder it's called Speed! I could hardly control myself, in fact I couldn't have if I had wanted to, and I didn't want to. I danced like I had never dreamed possible for introverted, mousy little me. I felt great, free, abandoned, a different, improved, perfected specimen of a different, improved, perfected species. It was wild! It was beautiful! It really was.

July 23

Dear Diary,

Gramps had a little heart attack last night, thank goodness it happened just as I was getting ready to go out and it wasn't really serious. Poor Gran is pretty much beside herself, but she's staying calm on the outside anyway. They haven't bugged me at all since I've been here, and they've been so delighted that I'm having a good time and that I've met a lot of friends that they stay completely out of my way. Dear-hearted square souls. If they only really knew what was happening! Their eyebrows would be shocked up into the middle of their heads.

Gramps' attack only means that he'll be bedridden for a few weeks, but I'll have to really be careful that I don't cause any extra trouble so that they'll want to send me home. Maybe if I start helping more around the house they'll even think they need me.

I hope nothing happens to Gramps. I love him so much. I know sometime both he and Gran will have to die, but I hope that isn't for a very long, long time yet. It's strange, but I've never thought much about dying till now. I suppose someday even I will have to die. I wonder if there really is a life after death. Oh, I do hope there is! But that isn't the part that really worries me. Actually I know that our souls will go back up to God, but when I think about our bodies being buried in the dark cold ground and being eaten by worms and rotting I can hardly stand the thought. I think I'd rather be cremated, yes, I would! I definitely would! I'm going to ask Mom and Dad and the kids as soon as I get home to be sure and have me cremated when I die. They will, they're a sweet and wonderful and good family and I love them and I'm lucky to have them. I must remember to write to them again this very day. I haven't been too good about writing, and I must, I simply must be better. And I think I'll tell them I want to come home, now! Right now! I want to get away from Bill and Jill and all the others. I don't know why I shouldn't use drugs, because they're wild and they're beautiful and they're wonderful, but I know I shouldn't, and I won't! I won't ever again. I hereby solemnly promise that I will from this very day forward live so that everyone I know can be proud of me and so that I can be proud of myself!

July 25

Gramps is getting along fine. I've done all the cooking and cleaning and everything so Gran could just stay with him all the time. They really appreciate it and I appreciate them.

6:30

Jill called and invited me to a party, but I told her I'm committed to my grandparents till things are better. I'm glad I had an excuse for not going.

July 28

Mom and Dad have been calling every day since Gramps had his attack. They asked me if I wanted to come home and I really do, but I feel I should stay here till at least next week and help.

August 2

I'm getting bored to the teeth, but at least I'm giving moral support to Gran, and after all she's done for me all my life that's the least I can do. Bill called again and asked me for a date and Gran insists that I get out so I guess I'll go with him but I'll just baby-sit if he wants to trip.

August 3

Bill had six kids over to his house last night. His folks had gone to the city so they wouldn't be back till one or two. They were all going to trip on acid, and since I'd been cooped up for so long I decided I might as well take one last trip too. I'm certainly not going to use any of the stuff when I get home. It was groovy, even greater than the others. I don't see how each trip can be better than the one before, but they are. I sat for hours examining the exoticness and magnificence of my right hand. I could see the muscles and the cells and the pores. Each blood vessel was a fascination unto itself, and my mind still flutters with the wonder of it all.

August 6

Well, last night it happened. I am no longer a virgin! In a way I'm really sorry, because I always wanted Roger to be the first and only boy in my life, but he's away visiting, in fact I haven't seen him since I got here. He might have grown into a gawky, stupid, rambling idiot anyhow.

I wonder if sex without acid could be so exciting, so wonderful, so indescribable. I always thought it just took a minute, or that it would be like dogs mating, but it wasn't like that at all. Actually, last night it took me a long time to get started on the trip. I just sat in the corner feeling left out and sort of antagonistic, then suddenly it happened and I wanted to dance wildly and make love. I hadn't known that I even felt that way about Bill. He had seemed a nice quiet person who took care of me when I needed support, but suddenly I didn't have any inhibitions about trying to seduce him, not that he needed much pressure. Actually it still doesn't seem quite real.

All my life I've thought that the first time I had sex

43

with someone it would be something special, and maybe even painful, but it turned out to be just part of the brilliant, freaky, way-out, forever pattern. I still can't quite separate one thing from another.

I wonder if all the kids had sex – but no, that's just too awfully animal and indecent! I wonder how shocked Roger would be if he knew, and my parents and Tim and Alex and Gramps and Gran? I think they would be mortified, but no more than I am!

Maybe I even really love Bill, but right now I can hardly even remember what he looks like. Oh, I'm so horribly, nauseously mixed up and – what if I'm pregnant? Oh, how I wish I had someone, anyone, to talk with who knows what they're talking about.

I hadn't thought about being pregnant before. Can it happen the first time? Will Bill marry me if I am or will he just think I'm an easy little dum-dum who makes it with everyone? Of course he won't marry me, he's only fifteen years old. I guess I'll just have to have an abortion or something. I certainly couldn't stand it if I had to leave school like _____ did last year. The kids talked about absolutely nothing else for weeks. Oh God, please, please make me not pregnant!

I'm going to call Mom right now. I'll get Gran to buy a plane ticket and I am going home tomorrow. I hate this rotten place and I hate Bill Thompson and all that crowd. I don't know how I ever got mixed up with them, but I was so pleased and felt so smart when they accepted me and now I feel miserable and ashamed as though that's going to do any good.

August 7

Mom and Dad think I should wait until next week to come home. I couldn't really argue, because Gran needs me. But in the meantime I'm not going to answer the phone or step off our property.

Later
Jill called, but I told Gran to tell her I wasn't feeling well. It's pretty obvious, even to Gran, that I'm really not. I'm living with doubts and apprehensions and fears that I never dreamed possible.

August 9

The world has actually stopped in its orbit. My life is completely over. After dinner when Gran and I were sitting out in the garden we heard tappings at the back gate and guess who of all the people in the universe stopped by? Roger and his mom and dad. They got back in the afternoon and heard about Gramps' sickness and had dropped by to visit him.

I was beside myself. Roger is even more breath-takingly good-looking than ever, and I wanted to throw myself in his arms and cry my heart out to him. Instead we shook hands and I hurried to get everybody something to drink. Later, after we'd all talked for a while, Gran sent me in to get some chips and dip, and Roger followed me! Can you imagine Roger following me? He even asked me out! I wanted to die right then and there, and later when we were out in the garden he started telling me about how he was going to military school for the next year and a half till he was ready for college. He even said he was a little frightened and lonely about going away by himself for the first time, and he told me how he wanted to become an aeronautical engineer and work on new techniques for air travel. He's got some wonderful ideas! It's almost like reading Jules Verne, and he has so many plans for his life, with the Army and all.

Then he kissed me and it was what I had always dreamed it would be since I was in kindergarten. Other boys have kissed me but it wasn't the same at all. This was fondness and liking and desire and regard and admiration and affection and tenderness and attachment and yearning. It was the most wonderful thing that has ever happened in my life. But now I'm sitting here and I feel sick to my stomach. What if he finds out about what I've been doing since I got here? How could he ever forgive me? How could he ever understand? Would he? If I were only a Catholic maybe I could do some kind of terrible penance to pay for my transgressions. I was brought up to believe that God would forgive people's sins, but how can I forgive myself? How could Roger forgive me?

Oh, terrors, horrors, endless torment.

August 10

Roger has called four times today but I refused to talk to him. Gran and Gramps want me to stay over a few days until I feel better but I *can't*. I simply can't face Roger again until I get my thinking straightened out. Oh, how did I ever get mixed up in such a mess? Imagine losing my virginity four nights before seeing Roger again. The awful irony of it! But even without that, would he have understood the acid trips? Would he have wanted me after those? I hadn't really cared before, but I care now! And it's too late!

I must talk to someone. I must find someone who

understands about drugs and talk to them. I wonder if I could talk to someone at Dad's university. Oh, no, no, they'd be bound to tell him and then I'd really be in a mess. Maybe I could say I was doing a paper on drugs for a science project or something, but I can't do that until school starts. I think I'd better take some of Gramps' sleeping pills, I'm never going to be able to sleep without them. In fact I think I'd better take a supply of them. He's got plenty, and I'm sure I'll have a few bad nights at home before I get straightened out. Oh, I hope it's just a few.

August 13

It's all I can do to keep from crying. Mom and Dad just called to say how proud they are to have me for a daughter. There are no words to express how I feel.

August 14

Gran took me to the plane. She thinks Roger and I had a quarrel. She kept telling me everything would be all right and that it is a woman's place to be long-suffering and patient and tolerant and understanding. Oh, if she only knew! Mom and Dad and Tim and Alex met me and all told me how pale and wan I looked, they were ever so gentle and loving. It's good to be home.

I must forget about everything. I must repent and forgive myself and start over; after all I just turned 15 and I can't stop life and get off. Besides since I've thought about Gramps dying I don't want to die. I'm afraid. Isn't that ghastly and ironic? I'm afraid to live and afraid to die, just like the old Negro spiritual. I wonder what their hang-up was?

August 16

Mother is making me eat. She's fixing all my favorite foods but they still don't taste like much. Roger wrote me a long letter asking me if I was all right, but I simply haven't the energy or the strength or the desire to answer him. Everyone is terribly worried about me and, in fact, I'm even terribly worried about myself. I still don't know if I'm pregnant and won't know for another ten or twelve days. Oh, I pray I'm not. I keep asking myself how I could have been such an idiot, and there is no answer other than the fact that I am an idiot! A stupid, bungling, senseless, foolish, ignorant idiot!

August 17

I have used the last of Gramps' sleeping pills and I'm a wreck. I can't sleep and I'm all screwed up and Mom is insisting that I go see Doctor Langley. Maybe that will help. I'll do anything.

August 18

I went to see Doctor Langley this morning and I really laid it on about my not being able to sleep. He asked me a lot of questions about why I couldn't sleep, but I just kept repeating I didn't know, I didn't know, I didn't know. Finally he broke down and gave me the pills. Actually I don't need the sleep as much as I need the escape. It's a wonderful way to escape. I think I can't stand it and then I just take a pill and wait for sweet nothingness to take over. At this stage in my life nothingness is a lot better than somethingness.

August 20

I don't think the sleeping pills Doctor Langley gave me are as strong as the ones Gramps had because I have to

50

take two of these and sometimes even three. Maybe it's because I'm so nervous. Anyway I don't know how much longer I can last; if something doesn't happen soon I think I'm going to blow my brains out.

August 22

I had Mom call Doctor Langley and I'm going to ask him for some tranquilizers. I can't sleep all day long and I certainly can't walk around like this so I hope he gives them to me. He's got to!

August 23

Tranquilizers are the greatest. This afternoon I took one just before the mailman's arrival with another letter from Roger. Instead of getting all upset, I sat down and poured my whole soul out to him, nothing of course about my acid trips or the Speed, and surely not about Bill and my possible condition, but just about the important things that concern us both. I have even begun to wonder if maybe I could turn Roger on just once so he would understand. Could I? Could I make him take his first trip unknowingly as I did?

Oh I wish I dared! It seems like I've been held down for so long, maybe it's the sleeping pills and the tranquilizers, but there are moments when I'd really like to just burst loose, but I guess those days are gone forever! I'm really confused! I wish I had someone to talk to!

August 26

What a wonderful, beautiful, happy day! My period started! I was never so happy for anything in my life. Now I can throw away my sleeping pills and tranquilizers, I can be me again! Oh, wow!

September 6

Beth came back from camp, but she's hardly the same person and she met some Jewish jerk that she's going steady with. They are going to be together all the time, day and night. Perhaps I'm a little jealous because Roger lives so far away and school has started and Alex and her noisy little friends are driving me crazy and Mom has begun to get on my back too.

Today I went down to this great little boutique and

found a cute pair of moccasins and a vest with fringe and a really great pair of pants. Chris, the girl who works there, showed me how to iron my hair (which I did tonight) and now it's perfectly straight. It's the greatest! The greatest except that Mom couldn't stand it. I went downstairs to show her and she said I look like a hippie and that she and Dad and I must have a little talk some evening. I could tell them a thing or two, because I imagine that sex without drugs isn't even the same thing as the mad, forever wonder of it when you're really way out there. Anyway I seem to be doing less and less right, I'm getting so that no matter what I do I can't please the Establishment.

September 7

Last night was the bitter end. Mom and Dad flowed tears and flowers about how much they love me and how worried they've been about my attitude since I got back from Gran's. They hate my hair, which they still want me to wear in a flip like the kiddies, and they talked and talked and talked, but never once did they even hear one thing I was trying to say to them. In fact at the beginning, when they were telling me about their deep concern, I had the overwhelming desire to break down and tell them everything. I wanted to tell them! I wanted more than anything in the world to know that they understood, but naturally they just kept on talking and talking because they are incapable of really understanding anything. If only parents would listen! If only they would let us talk instead of forever and eternally and continuously harping and preaching and nagging and correcting and yacking, yacking, yacking! But they won't listen! They simply won't or can't or don't want to listen, and we kids keep winding up back in the same old frustrating, lost, lonely corner with no one to relate to either verbally or physically. However, I'm lucky I have Roger, if I really have him.

September 9

Another sock in the belly day. Roger is definitely going to that military school and the first time he'll be home is Christmas – and maybe not even then! His dad went there and his grandfather did too, so I guess he's almost obligated to go, but I need him here, not there in that idiot school marching around for a whole year. Now we'll be a whole continent away. I wrote him a ten page letter telling him I'll wait for him even though in his last letter he told me that he expected me to date and have fun. But how can I have fun in this hole????

September 10

I was so depressed about Roger that I walked down to look at clothes in the boutique where Chris works. It was almost her coffee break so we went next door to have a coke and I told her how low I was because of Roger. She immediately understood. It was great to have someone again that I could talk to. When we got back to the store she gave me a little red candy type thing and told me to go home, take it and listen to some groovy music. She said, 'This heart will pep you up like tranquilizers slow you down,' and you know she was right! I've been using too many sleeping pills and too many tranquilizers. I don't know why that dumb doctor didn't give me something to make me feel better instead of something to make me feel worse. I've been feeling great all afternoon, feeling like living again. I've washed my hair and cleaned my room and ironed and done all the things that Mom has been nagging me to do for days. The only problem is that now it's night and I can't seem to turn the energy off. I'd stay up and write to Roger, but I just wrote him a giant letter yesterday and he'd think I was some kind of nut. I guess I'll just have to waste one of my good sleeping pills to stop it. That's life.

See ya.

September 12

Dad and Mom are constantly harping about the way I look. They keep saying that they know I'm a good, sweet girl, but I'm beginning to act like a hippie and they're afraid the wrong kind of people will be drawn to me. What it amounts to is they are so ultra-conservative that they don't even know what's happening. Chris and I talk a lot about our parents and the Establishment. Her dad is an executive with a breakfast food company and he travels a lot 'often in the company of other women' she confided to me. And her mom is such a devoted club and civic-minded woman that the whole town would probably fall flat on its face if she took an evening off to listen to her daughter. 'Mom's the "pillar of society" in this town,' Chris told me. 'She holds up everybody and everything but me, and man have I been let down.'

Chris doesn't need to work but she just simply can't stand it around her house. I told her I was beginning to feel the same way and she's going to try and get me a job with her, isn't that the greatest?

September 13

Wow! I'm really living! I have a job. Chris asked her boss last night and he said yes. Isn't that the greatest?! I'll be working with Chris on Thursday nights and on Friday nights and all day Saturday and I'll be able to buy anything my non-conforming little heart desires. Chris is a year older than I am and she's a year ahead in school, but she really is a great girl and I love her and relate better to her than I ever have with anyone in my life, even Beth. I suspect she knows a little about drugs, because she's given me hearts a couple of times when I've been really low. Someday soon I've really got to talk to her about these things.

September 21

Dear friend Diary,

I'm sorry I've been neglecting you, but I really have been busy with my new job and school starting and all, and you still are my very dearest friend and closest confidant, even though I am really tuned in and receive well with Chris. We never get tired and she and I are two of the most popular girls at school. I know I look great, I'm still down at 103 pounds, and every time I get hungry or tired I just pop a Benny. We've got energy and vitality to spare, and clothes, like man. My hair is the greatest. I wash it in mayonnaise and it's shining and soft enough to make anyone turn on.

I still haven't met a guy I really dig, but that's probably all right because I'm waiting for Roger.

September 23

Diary,

My parents are absolutely and positively going to make me blow my mind. I have to take Dexies to stay high at school and at work and on dates and to do my homework, then I have to take tranquilizers to bear up at home. Daddy thinks I'm blowing his image as the college dean. He even yelled at me at the table last night for saying 'man.' He has *his* words when he wants to stress a point and that is all right, but let me say 'man,' and you'd think I had committed the unpardonable sin.

Chris and I are about ready to cut out. She has a friend in San Francisco who could help us get a job, and since we've both had experience in a boutique it shouldn't be that hard. Besides her parents are about ready for a divorce. They do nothing but fight when they are together and she's had it. At least I don't have to put up with that.

Also Roger says he's too busy to write much, which is an unlikely story. Like Chris says, 'a man's blood soon runs cold when there is no one around to warm it up.'

September 26

Last night was the night, friend! I finally smoked pot and it was even greater than I expected! Last night after work, Chris fixed me up with a college friend of hers who knew I'd been on acid, etc., but who wanted to turn me on to hash.

He told me not to expect to feel like I felt with liquor and I told him I'd never had more than champagne at birthday parties and leftovers from cocktail parties. We all got hilarious over that and Ted, Chris's date, said that lots of kids never try booze, not only because it's their parents' thing, but because it's a lot harder to get than pot. Ted said that when he first started experimenting he found he could steal a lot of money from his parents and they would never miss it, but let him take one swig out of any of their booze bottles and it was as though they had it measured to the ounce.

Then Richie showed me how to smoke. And I've never even had a cigarette! He gave me a small orientation lecture, like I should listen for small things I wouldn't ordinarily hear and just relax. At first I took too deep a drag and almost choked to death, so Richie told me to suck in openmouthed gulps to mix as much air in as possible. But that didn't work too well either and after a while Ted gave up and brought out a hookah pipe. It seemed funny and exotic but at first I couldn't get any smoke and I felt cheated because the other three were obviously stoned. But finally it started to work, just when I thought it never would, and I really began to feel happy and free as a bright canary chirping through the open, endless heavens. And I was so relaxed! I don't think I've been that relaxed in my whole entire life! It was really beautiful. Later Rich brought a sheepskin rug out of his room and we began walking through the thickness of it and there was a sensation in my feet that was totally indescribable, a softness that enveloped my complete body, and quite suddenly I could hear the strange almost silent sound of the long silky hairs rubbing against each other and against my feet. It was a sound unsimilar to any I have ever heard, and I remember trying desperately to give a dissertation upon the phenomena of each individual hair having perfect pitch within itself. But of course I couldn't; it was too perfect.

Then I picked up a salted peanut and noticed that nothing had ever tasted so salty before. It felt like being a child again and trying to swim in the Great Salt Lake. Only the peanut was even saltier! My liver and my spleen and my intestines were corroded with salt. I longed to taste a fresh peach or strawberry and have the flavor and sweetness and delectibleness of them consume me also. It was great and I began to laugh in a totally mad way. I was delighted that I was so different. Everyone in the whole universe was mad except me. I was the only sane and perfect being. Somewhere in my brain I remembered reading that a thousand years with man is as a day with the Lord and I had found the answer. I was even now in my new time length living the lives of a thousand men in the space of hours.

Later we were all very thirsty and dying for something sweet. So we walked to the ice cream shop, joking about the incredible high curbs and the unbelievable oddly shaped moon which kept changing shapes and colors. I don't know if we were all really as high as we said we were, but it was fun. And in the restaurant, we joked and laughed as though the whole world and its secrets belonged to us alone. When Richie brought me home about midnight, my parents (who were both up) were very pleased with the nice, young, clean-cut gentlemanly young man I was going out with. They didn't even complain about what time it was! Can you believe it?

P.S. Richie gave me some joints to smoke when I'm alone and I want to be in heaven. Isn't that nice, nice, nice!

October 5

Chris and I are thinking about quitting our jobs because it's getting so that we don't have any time for what *we* want to do.

I'm deeply in love with Richie, and Chris is in love with Ted, and we want to spend as much time with them as we can. The bitch is that none of us ever seem to have enough money, so Chris and I have both had to push a little pot. Of course we only sell to the kids who are heavy users and who would just buy it from someone else if they didn't get it from us.

Ted and Richie are in college, and they have to work a lot harder than we do in high school so they don't have the time to sell. And besides it's a lot easier for guys to get busted than for girls. At first it was pretty hard to keep my cool around the Establishment, but since I'm now Richie's chick all the way I have to do what I can to help him.

October 8

I convinced Rich that it would be easier to push acid than pot, at least we can put it on penny stamps or gum or life savers and carry them around with us without having the fuzz breathing down our necks or without having some idiot fink find out where or what our bag is.

Richie is so good, good, good to me and sex with him is like lightning and rainbows and springtime. I may be just chipping around with drugs, but I'm really hooked on that boy. We would do absolutely anything for each other. He's going into medicine, and I've got to help him any way I can. It's going to be a long hard pull but we'll make it. Imagine eight or ten more years of school for him – and he's already in his second year of college! Mom and Dad think he's still in high school. I think I won't go on to college. Dad will just curl up and die, but it's more important for me to work and help Rich. As soon as I'm out of high school I'll get a full time job and we'll settle down. He's been a straight A student but he says he's slipping a little.

I really love that man. Oh, I really truly do! I can't wait to get to him. He teases me and says I'm oversexed because I've been bugging him to let me try sex without being stoned first. He's promised me he will. It will be almost like a new experience. I can hardly wait.

(?)

Richie and I never go anywhere. It's almost a ritual for him to pick me up, and spend a few minutes with my parents and then rush over to the apartment he shares with Ted. I really wish we could be together stoned every night, but he only lets me come over when he restocks my acid supply and gives me enough grass and barbs to last me until I see him again. I know he's studying very hard so I try to content myself with what he can give me of himself which seems to be getting less and less. Maybe I am oversexed, at least I seem to be a lot more interested in it than he is. But that's only because he worries so about me. I wish he'd let me take the pill and I wish he didn't have to work and study so hard. Oh, well, what I've got is so great I don't know how I could even wish for anything more.

October 17

Today I went to the grade school again. I don't mind pushing at high school because the stuff is sometimes kind of hard to get and the kids usually come up and ask me for it. Chris and I just supply it from Richie. He can get whatever is their bag, barbs or pot or amphetamines or LSD or DMT or meth or anything. The high school kids are one thing and even the junior high, but today I sold ten stamps of LSD to a little kid at the grade school who was not even nine years old, I'm sure. I know that he in turn must be pushing and these kids are just too young! The thought of nine and ten year olds getting wasted is so repulsive that I'm not going over there anymore! I know if they want it they'll get it somewhere but they won't get it from me! I've been lying here on my bed ever since I got home from school thinking about it, and I've decided that Richie must come over and see Dad about a scholarship, surely with his grades and background something could be worked out. I'm sure it could.

October 18

If there were medals and prizes for stupidity and gullibleness I certainly would receive the half-assed one. Chris and I walked into Richie and Ted's apartment to find the bastards stoned and making love to each other. No wonder Richie Bitchie wanted so little to do with me! Here I am out peddling drugs for a low class queer whose dad probably isn't sick at all. I wonder how many other dumb chicks he's got working for him? Oh, I'm so ashamed! I can't believe I've sold to eleven and twelve year olds and even nine and ten year olds. What a disgrace I am to myself and my family and to everybody. I'm as bad as that sonofabitch Richie.

October 19

Chris and I sat around the park all day thinking things over. She's been using drugs for over a year and I've been on since July 10 to be exact. We've decided it would be impossible to change while we're here so we're going to cut out and go to San Francisco. And I've simply got to turn Richie in to the police. I'm not being vindictive or spiteful or jealous, really I'm not. It's just that I've got to do something to protect all those grade and junior high school kids.

All this crap Rich sold me about 'they'll get it someplace' and all that is just a bunch of high pressure bullshit. He doesn't care about any one in this whole world but himself, and the only way I can make retribution for what I've done is to at least keep him from getting more kids started. That's one of the worst things about this drug business. Practically every kid that uses also sells and it's just a giant round robin thing that keeps on getting bigger and bigger until I wonder where it will ever end! I really do! I wish I'd never gotten started. And now Chris and I have both pledged to each other that we're going to stay clean. We really and truly are! We've given our sacred oath and promise. In San Francisco we won't know a single soul that uses it and it will be easy to stay off.

(?)

It's very sad sneaking off in the middle of the night, but Chris and I could think of no other way. The bus will be leaving at 4:30 A.M. and we must be on it. First we'll go to Salt Lake City for a while and then backtrack to San Francisco. I am really quite afraid of what Richie might do if he caught me. He will almost surely know the one who turned him in because I told the police in my letter about the few places I know where he stashes his supply. I wish all dealers could be put away!

Goodbye dear home, goodbye good family. I really am leaving mostly because I love you so much and I don't want you to ever know what a weak and disreputable person I have been. And I hate being a high school dropout, but I dare not even write for my transcripts, knowing you and Richie might follow them. I'm leaving you a note beloved family, but it can never tell you how sacred you are to me.

October 26

We are in San Francisco, in a dirty smelling and stifling little one room apartment. We are both filthy after so many miserable hours on the bus, and since Chris is taking her bath down the hall I will write a few lines till it is my turn. I'm sure we have enough money to last us till we get jobs because I kept the one hundred and thirty dollars I was supposed to turn in to bastard Richie, and Chris was able to draw out the four hundred plus dollars she had in the bank. This whoring little spider hole we are in cost ninety dollars for the month, but at least that will give us enough time to get jobs and look for a decent place to live.

I feel dreadful about my parents, but at least they know I'm with Chris and they think she is a nice and respectable girl who won't lead me astray. Boy, how much further astray could I go?

October 27

Chris and I have looked all day for jobs. We've followed up every ad in the paper, but we're either too young, or too inexperienced, or we don't have references, or they want someone with a following, or they'll call us. I have never been so damned exhausted in my life. We certainly won't need anything to make us sleep tonight, even on the lumpy, soggy, let down contraption which is called a bed in this cracker box.

October 28

Everything always feels clammy and damp here. There is even a green type of fungus mold growing in the closet, but thank goodness we won't be here long, at least I *hope* we won't be here long! But today was no more successful than yesterday in job hunting. We couldn't locate Chris's friend either.

October 29

I took a job in some crappy little lingerie store. It doesn't pay much, but at least it will keep us in groceries, etc. Chris will keep looking for a better job and after she gets one then I will quit and look for something a little more challenging. Chris hopes that maybe in a year we can open our own boutique. Wouldn't that be wonderful? And maybe when we're very successful we can invite our families to come and see us and glory in our success.

October 31

Chris still doesn't have a job. She looks every day but we both decided that she wouldn't take just anything. It has to be in a first rate store where she can learn everything we'll need to know to run our own place. Every night I am so tired I can hardly make it to bed. I didn't realize that standing up all day waiting on grouchy, lousy people would be so exhausting.

November 1

Chris and I spent the day touring Chinatown and Golden Gate Park and we took a bus across the bridge. It's a wonderful and exciting and beautiful city, but I really wish I were home. Of course I couldn't tell Chris that.

November 3

Chris finally has a job! It's in the greatest little shop I've ever seen. I went down after work and bought a pair of sandals. She can learn everything there is to know about buying and displaying as well as selling, because there are only two of them in the shop. Shelia is the owner, and she is without a doubt the most fabulous looking woman I have ever seen. Skin as clear and white as snow and eyelashes as long as my arm, fake of course. Her hair is jet black and I know that she is all of six feet tall. I can't understand why she isn't modeling or in movies or on TV. Her shop is in a very exclusive little area and her prices are high, high, high, even with Chris's discount, but anyway I just felt I had to splurge after all the scrimping we've done and are going to continue to do.

November 5

I'm getting more homesick every day instead of more weaned away. I wonder how Chris feels? I don't dare say anything for fear she will think I'm a big boob, which I probably am. Actually I think I'd go on home if I weren't so afraid of Richie. I'm sure he'd try to involve me if he could. He's such a weak, conniving, vindictive character. I see so many things about him now that are repulsive that I don't know how I ever got so miserably brainwashed. Guess I was just a stupid, dumb kid asking to be taken, and I was! Man, was I ever! But next time I won't be so stupid, except there won't be any next time! I will never ever, ever, under any circumstances use drugs again. They are the root and cause of this whole rotten, stinking mess I am in, and I wish with all my heart and soul that I had never heard of them. And I wish letters didn't carry postmarks, then I could write to Mom and Dad and the kids and Gran and Gramps and maybe even Roger. There are so many things I would like to tell them. It's just too bad I didn't realize it in time.

November 8

Get up, eat, work, eat, and fall into bed exhausted. I don't even take a bath every day anymore, it's too much trouble to wait around for the bathroom to be empty.

November 10

I quit my job and I'm going to spend my full time looking for a more interesting one. Shelia had a list of places to which I can go and says I can use her name as a reference.

P.S. We splurged and got a second-hand TV for $15. It doesn't work too well but it cheers the place up.

November 11

Well Diary,

How do you like this, I got a job my very first hour out, in fact it was the second shop I went to! Mario Mellani makes exquisite custom jewelry, much of it filled with precious stones. He wanted someone young and fresh-looking to be kind of window dressing and background for his work. I am flattered that he chose me! Mr Mellani is big and fat and jolly and tells me he has a wife and eight children who live in Sausalito and already he has invited me over some Sunday for dinner, and to meet them.

November 13

I adore my new job. Mr Mellani is like a second family to me. Here he is in this very exclusive little shop in the lobby of an incredibly expensive hotel, yet he brings his lunch every day in a paper sack and shares it with me. He says it keeps him from getting too fat. And Chris and I are going out to his home on Sunday! Isn't that great! It will be really wonderful to see a bunch of little kids again. He has one son Roberto just Tim's age and another little boy only three days younger than Alexandria. He thinks I am an orphan and I really am in a way. Oh, well.

You know, I could have plenty of dates if I weren't particular. Our lobby is swarming with wealthy old fat men and their wealthy, mink and sable and chinchillad old wives. The men stash their wives up in their suites then come down and make passes at me. There are also endless numbers of traveling salesmen types who wander through trying to handle more than the merchandise, it hasn't taken me many days to learn how to spot them as they pass the first doorman.

(?)

Chris and I are lucky that both our shops are closed on Sundays and Mondays so we have our two free days together. There aren't too many really young people like us around. Shelia must be a terrifically preserved thirty and of course Mr Mellani is old enough to be my father, and a father he is fast becoming. Tomorrow we go to his house.

November 16

We really had a fascinating time at Mr Mellani's. They live in a little hillside area which almost seems country. It's at the very end of the bus line and all covered with big ageless trees. Mrs Mellani and the kids are just like the Italian families in the movies, and she cooks like nothing I've ever eaten before. And the kids, even the big kids, crawl continuously all over their parents. I've never seen such a physical bunch. Mario, the big seventeen-year-old, was going on some kind of field trip and he kissed and hugged his father as well as the rest of the family as though he were going away forever. The rest of the day was also generously sprinkled with physical spats and spanks and slaps.

It was a lovely experience which only made me more lonely.

November 19

Chris came home from work elated. Shelia, not to be outdone by Mr Mellani, invited us to a party she's having at her house Saturday night after work. It will start a little late as all of us work till nine, but I'm glad because it sounds terribly glamorous and sophisticated to be going to a party at 10:30 P.M.

November 20

At first Chris and I were worried about what we would wear to Shelia's, but she told us just to wear something comfortable, which is great because we only brought one suitcase each from home and we're really not in the mood to spend if we don't have to. I think maybe we'll stay in this apartment for another six months or so then we'll probably have enough money to start on our own. I hope Shelia will give us her blessings and help us. Maybe Mr Mellani will let us handle some of his cheaper things too. Mario is going to come work in the shop as soon as he graduates from high school, so maybe they wouldn't need me anyway.

November 21

Tomorrow is Shelia's party. I wonder who will be there? Chris is always telling me about the movie and TV people who come in that Shelia seems to know personally. At least they all kiss each other and call everybody 'darling' or 'baby.'

Imagine knowing movie stars and TV stars personally! _____ came into Mr Mellani's shop one day and bought a big dinner ring, but she's so old that I've only seen her in one late, late movie on TV and she played a not too exciting or glamorous crazy woman.

November 22

Oh happy Saturday. Tonight is the sophisticated night. I wonder if they'll think I'm terribly naive if I drink coke or something instead of champagne or whatever they have. Maybe no one will even notice. I better dash off to work, sometimes my cable car is packed at this time of day and I don't want to have to hang on the outside and get my hair all stringy.

November 23

It has happened again and I don't know whether to weep or rejoice. Well, at least this time we were all adults doing our adult thing and not influencing a bunch of little kids. Granted some people wouldn't consider me quite an adult, but everyone thinks both Chris and I are eighteen so I guess that's all that matters. Anyway, Shelia lives in the most fabulous apartment with the most spectacular view. She has a doorman who is even more regal looking than the doormen where I work – and they are pretty impressive. We took the elevator up to her apartment, trying to act sophisticated and un-impressed when actually after our dirty little fly trap both of us were panting. Even the elevator was impressive with gold vinyl paper on two sides and black paneling on the other two.

Shelia's apartment was like walking into a decorating magazine. Two whole walls were glass overlooking the twinkling city. I tried to keep my mouth from hanging open, but it was like finding myself on a movie set.

Shelia kissed us each lightly on our cheeks and led us into the room where brightly colored pillows were stacked around a large gold and antiqued mirrored coffee table. There was an oversized buff colored shaggy fur chair next to the fireplace, and the whole thing was really too much.

Then the doorbell was ringing and the most beautiful human beings I have ever seen in my life began arriving. The men were so gorgeous, they were like tanned statues of the Roman Gods, and the women were so breathtaking that it made me happy and frightened all at the same time. But after a while it dawned on me that we're young and shiny and healthy and these women are old, old, old. They probably couldn't even go out of the house in the morning without a half a ton of makeup on. So we really didn't have anything to worry about at all.

Then I smelled it. I almost stopped talking in the middle of a sentence, the smell was so strong. Chris was over on the other side of the room but I saw her looking around and knew she had smelled it too. The air seemed to be getting thick and parts of my head were begging for it. I didn't know whether to run or stay or what. Then I turned around and one of the men passed me a joint and that was it. I wanted to be ripped, smashed, torn up as I had never wanted anything before. This was the scene, these were the swingers and I wanted to be part of it!

The rest of the evening was fantastic. The lights and music and sound and San Francisco were part of me and I was part of them. It was another incredible excursion and it went on for I don't know how long. Chris and I both used Shelia's apartment for a crashpad, and it was early afternoon before we pulled ourselves together enough to go back to our own dingy four walls.

I'm a little worried about what actually happened. I don't know if we were smoking hash, which is hard to get right now, or what. But I hope I won't have to go through this am-I-or-aren't-I-until-next-month bit again. One thing – if we are going to get back on the merry-go-round I really am going to start taking the pill. I can't stand the suspense, and besides now all I need to topple completely would be to find myself . . . but I won't even think about it.

(?)

Shelia has parties almost every night and we are always invited. I haven't found anyone I'm really into yet but it's fun, fun, fun and we nearly always use her place as a crashpad – which is a lot better than having to come back to this hole we're in. Chris found out that Shelia was once married to _____ and her alimony is enough to support her and all her friends in any habit they happen to have. Boy, wouldn't it be nice to have money like that!!! I think I'd live just the way she does, only better.

December 3

Last night was the worst night of my shitty, rotten, stinky, dreary fucked-up life. There were only four of us, and Shelia and Rod, her current 'boyfriend,' introduced us to heroin. At first we were a little afraid, but they convinced us that the horror stories were just so many American myths – ha! But I guess I was pretty excited and the truth is I really couldn't wait when I was watching them set up. Smack is a great sensation, different from anything I'd ever had before. I felt gentle and drowsy and wonderfully soft like I was floating above reality and the mundane things were lost forever in space. But just before I was too out of it to notice what was going on, I saw Shelia and that cocksucker she goes with lighting up and setting out Speed. I remember wondering why were they getting high when they had just set us out on this wonderful low, and it wasn't until later I realized that the dirty sonsofbitches had taken turns raping us and treating us sadistically and brutally. That had been their planned strategy all along, the low-class shit eaters.

When Chris and I finally came down, we crippled our way back to the apartment and talked for a long time. We've had it! The garbage that goes with drugs makes the price too goddamned high for anyone to pay. This time we are really going to watch out for each other and help each other. I had condemned Richie for being a frigging homo, but maybe I should give even that mother a break. With the shit he was on everyday, it's no wonder he was out of control.

Still December 3

Chris and I talked again and have decided to leave this screwed-up scene. We've got seven hundred dollars counting yesterday's pay, so we can maybe start a boutique in some not too great area. We're certainly not going to chipper around anymore. We've both had enough of that!

I hate to leave Mr Mellani. He's been so kind and good and considerate of me, but neither Chris nor I can even stand the thought of seeing or hearing from that sadistic switch hitter Shelia again . . . So I guess I'll just leave another 'thanks' and 'I love you' note.

December 5

We've been spending ten hours a day looking for a place with no luck, now we've decided maybe we should start a shop over close to Berkeley. All the kids there wear lots of jewelry, and at least Chris got some of the suppliers' names before she left, and I'm sure that I can do some original things just from having watched Mr Mellani. That should make it a really fun shop with Chris doing the buying and the selling and me doing some original work.

December 6

Well, today we found it – our new home. It's a tiny ground floor apartment really close to Berkeley, which has now become a commercial district so we can use the kitchen and bedroom for living, and the living room and the microscopic dining room for our show room and a workshop. Tomorrow we move in and start painting. We have a nice bay window only a few feet from the street which will make a fantastic display window, and if we repaint and recover the furniture it actually won't be too bad. We're going to do all sorts of mad things, like covering the old worn tabletops with felt, which is cheap, and putting fake leopard on the chairs and on part of one wall if we can afford it. It will be good to have a place to call home again and this one we'll fix up to look loved and lived in. We didn't spend one single penny on the other apartment.

December 9

I have been too busy to write. We have been working twenty hours a day. We both laugh about how much we would like a Dexie but neither one of us will weaken ever again. We haven't done a thing to our living quarters but our show room looks adorable. Already a number of kids have stopped by to tell us how great it looks and to ask us when we'll be open. We couldn't afford carpeting so we've painted the floor candy cane pink and the walls we've done in pinks and white with all the accents in a warm soft red and purple. It looks simply great. Instead of using leopard we decided to use fake white fur and it's simply scrumptious. Chris has been down at the wholesale houses all day and tomorrow we open with or without sleep.

December 10

Apparently Chris knew just what to buy because just today we've done twenty dollars worth of business. She's going to have to go back to the market tomorrow.

December 12

The plumbing leaks and the toilet gets stopped up and we only have hot water part of the time, but it really doesn't matter. Kids stop by to watch our TV which we have in the show room or just to sit around and rap. We cut the legs off the dining room chairs so they are only about a foot from the floor and with the five of them (one was broken beyond repair) we've got a nice little conversation area. Today one of the kids suggested we stock our refrigerator with a few cold drinks and then charge 50¢ for them with TV privileges. I think we're going to try it. In fact we've even considered getting a cheap second-hand stereo in a few weeks if things continue to go well. Our show room is really quite large and we really only need half of it for business.

Most of the kids seem to have plenty of money and they buy enough to surely allow them chair privileges for a while.

December 13

Today one of the boys who's been in a number of times offered to sell us his stereo for twenty-five dollars because he's going to build a new one. We were elated and are staying up tonight to refinish it with red velvet and gold thumbtacks. Won't the kids be surprised tomorrow! I'm glad I'm always so tired I fall asleep the minute I touch the bed, because I don't want time to think, especially about Christmas.

December 15

This morning Chris left early to go to the wholesalers and I was listening to the stereo while I cleaned up the showcases. Then 'She's Leaving Home,' began playing, and before I knew what was happening I had tears dripping down my face like two spigots had been turned on inside my head. Oh that song was written about me and all the others of thousands of girls like me trying to escape. Maybe after Christmas I'll go home, maybe even before Christmas. This whole mess with Richie must surely be cleared up and I can go back and start in school at half year. Chris can have the whole shop and we should be fairly well established by then, or maybe she'll want to go home with me, but I won't even mention it for a while.

December 17

It's beginning to get a little monotonous for Chris and me. All the kids want to talk about is their hangups and how they feel when they're using. I remember Dad's father before he died talking on endlessly about his aches and his pains. These kids are beginning to hit at me the same way. They never talk about what they want out of life, or their families or anything, just who's holding, how much bread they'll get next year, and who has the least crumbs, at the moment, and will they cover. And the 'crazies' are beginning to get to me too. I wonder if we really are going to have a full scaled revolution in this country. When they're discussing it, it all seems pretty reasonable and exciting – destroying everything and starting again; a new country, a new love and sharing and peace. But when I'm alone it seems like another insane drugged scene. Oh, I'm so utterly confused. I can't believe that soon it will have to be mother against daughter and father against son to make the new world. But maybe they'll wear me down to their way of thinking by the time I'm in college, if I ever get there.

December 18

Today we just closed our doors and took off. It's the first time we've both had out together in weeks and the kids and their hang-ups were really beginning to bug us. We took a long leisurely bus ride and then splurged on an expensive many-coursed French dinner. It even felt good to be dressed up again after all the beating around in old pants and work clothes. But all the Christmas things in the windows and the stores make us both a little lonely inside although neither one of us says anything. I was even trying to pretend to myself that I wasn't affected, but I guess to you dear Diary I can tell the truth. I'm lonely, I'm heartbroken, I hate this whole number and everything it stands for, I feel I'm wasting my life away. I want to go back to my family and my school. I don't want to just sit listening to other kids who can go home for Christmas and who can write and phone when I can't and why can't I? I probably haven't done anything that these kids haven't done. All dopers are part-time sewer dwellers, the two go hand in hand together.

December 22

I called Mom. She was so glad to hear me I could hardly understand her through the tears. She offered to wire me money or have Daddy come and get me, but I told her we had enough and that we'd be back tonight on the first plane. Why didn't we do this weeks, months, centuries ago? Stupid us!

December 23

Last night was like reaching heaven. The plane was late but Mom and Dad and Tim and Alexandria were all there to meet me, and we were all crying unashamedly and like babies. Gran and Gramps are flying in today to see me and to stay for Christmas. I guess it's the greatest homecoming anyone ever had. I feel like the prodigal son being welcomed back into the fold, and I shall never ever go away again.

Chris's mother and dad met her and they too were reunited in a downpour of tears. Chris's leaving had one good result. It brought her mom and dad back together as they said they hadn't been in years.

Later

I'm so grateful that Chris and I were successful in our little venture. Mark, one of the boys who hung out at our shop, took colored Polaroid shots which have quite impressed our families. Of course we've deleted from our lives our adventures in San Francisco, and Mom was pleased that we never did even get down to Haight-Ashbury, which is nothing now anyway.

This afternoon I called the operator and asked for phone numbers for both Richie and Ted, but she didn't have a listing for either one. So I guess they've just dropped out of sight and I'm relieved. Now everyone just thinks we ran away because we wanted to be out on our own. I think I'll check to see if they are still registered in school, just to make sure.

December 24

The house is alive with fragrance. We have baked cakes and pies and cookies and candies. Gran is a wonderful cook and I know I can learn many things from her and I'm really going to try. The tree is up and the house is trimmed and Christmas is going to be even greater this year than it has been before.

I called Chris today and she feels great. Her mom and dad and her crippled Aunt Doris who lives there are really going out of their way to be nice to her. Oh, it's good to be home! I guess Mom was right, Chris and I used to dwell on the negative things. But not anymore!

December 25

Diary, today is Christmas and I am waiting for my family to wake up so that we can go empty our stockings and unwrap our presents. But first, and all by myself, I wanted to have my own special and sacred little part of this special and sacred day. I wanted to review and repent and recommit myself. Now I can sing with the others, 'Oh come all ye faithful, joyful and triumphant,' for I am triumphant, this time I really am!

December 26

The day after Christmas is usually a let down, but this year I enjoyed helping Mother and Gran clean up and put away and take out. I feel grown-up. I am no longer in the category with the children, I am one of the adults! And I love it! They have accepted me as an individual, as a personality, as an entity. I belong! I am important! I am somebody!

Adolescents have a very rocky insecure time. Grown-ups treat them like children and yet expect them to act like adults. They give them orders like little animals, then expect them to react like mature, and always rational, self-assured persons of legal stature. It is a difficult, lost, vacillating time. Perhaps I have passed over the worst part. I certainly hope so, because I surely would not have either the strength or the fortitude to get through that number again.

December 27

Christmas is still in the air. That something wonderful, something special time of year, when all things good are reborn upon earth. Oh, I love it, I love it, I love it. It is as though I have never been away.

December 28

I was looking through the Christmas cards and saw one from Roger's folks. How dreadful that makes me feel. Wouldn't it have been wonderful if their family and ours could have been related? But all possibility for that is now over and I must not torture myself. Besides it was probably only puppy love stuff.

December 29

Mom and Dad are planning a New Year's party for all the people connected with Dad's department. It sounds like fun. Gran is making her terrific broccoli and chicken casserole and she is also making her yeast orange rolls. Yum! She has promised to let me help her and Chris is coming over too.

December 30

It's still holiday time and I'm elated all the livelong day and night!

December 31

Tonight will ring in a wonderful new year for me. How humbly grateful I am to be rid of the old one. It hardly seems real! I wish I could just tear it out of my life like pages from the calendar, at least the last six months. How, oh how, could it ever have happened to me? Me, from this good and fine and upstanding, loving family! But the new year is going to be different, filled with life and promise. I wish there were some way to literally and truly and completely and permanently blot my for real nightmares out, but since there isn't, I must poke them way back into the darkest and most inaccessible corners and crevices of my brain, where perhaps they will eventually be covered over or become lost. But enough of this chitty-chat and writie-write, I've gotta go downstairs and help Mom and Gran. We've got a million things to do before the party. Up, up and away.

January 1

Last night's party was really fun. I hadn't thought Dad's friends could be so interesting, and funny. Some of the men were talking about outrageous cases that have been tried in court and the unbelievable decisions that have been handed down. One old eccentric multi-millionairess left every single cent of her money to two old overgrown alley cats who wore diamond encrusted collars while they scrambled around the house and prowled through the alleys. Part of her will specified that the cats not be controlled in any manner that would be against their natural instincts. So the court hired four full time cat sitters to watch them every minute of the day and night. I suspect the men who were telling the story exaggerated because it was so hilarious, but I'm not sure. Maybe they were just good storytellers.

Some of the parents talked about the cuckoo things their kids have done, and Dad even proudly told some good things about me . . . imagine!

At midnight everyone put on paper hats and rang bells and gongs, etc., then we had our midnight supper, with Gran and Chris and Tim and me all helping.

We didn't get to bed until almost four o'clock, but that was almost the best part. After all the guests left, the family and Chris and me all put on our pajamas and finished up the dishes and straightened up the house as relaxed and happy as anybody could possibly be. Gramps was washing the dishes with soapsuds up to his armpits and singing at the top of his voice. He insisted that the dishwasher was too slow when we had so many things to do, and Dad was prancing around and bringing in things and licking his fingers. It was really great! I wonder if the real guests had as much fun as Mom and Dad, and Gran and Gramps and Tim and I had had? Would Chris have preferred being with her own family if they hadn't been out to another party? I guess those are just a few of the things we'll never know, which aren't important anyway.

January 4

Tomorrow I start school again. It seems like I've been gone ages, instead of just part of one term. But I will appreciate it now, I can tell you. I'm going to learn to Habla Español like a Spaniard. I used to think foreign languages were dumb, but now I realize that it's very important to be able to communicate with people, with all people.

January 5

Chris is a senior, but we still had lunch together. It's kind of a hassle getting resettled.

January 6

What a shock! Today Joe Driggs came up and asked if I was holding. I had really almost forgotten that so short a time ago I was a pusher. Oh, I hope the word doesn't get any further, and that I can live it down. Actually Joe wouldn't believe at first that I was clean. He was really in a bad way and begged me for some chalk or anything. I hope George doesn't get the word.

January 7

Nothing was said today about drugs. I hope Joe gets the word back.

January 8

Chris and I have both been informed about a party this weekend but I've asked Mom if Chris can spend that time with me. I'm sure I won't be tempted, but I just don't want to take any chances. And I've also very truthfully (at least *part* truthfully) told Mom that a bunch of pretty fast kids are pushing us at school and we'd like family support for the next few weeks. Mom was most grateful that I had even confided in her and said she and Dad would try to plan something special for the next couple of weekends and see if Chris's folks wouldn't do the same for the two weeks after that. It was a nice warm feeling knowing that we were communicating, and much more than vocally! I really have a great family!

January 11

Our family and Chris spent the weekend in the mountains. It was everything that it possibly could have been! Dad borrowed the cabin from someone he works with and after we'd found out how to turn on the water and the furnace and everything it was really great. It snowed during the night and we all had to take turns shoveling out the car, but it was really lovely. Dad says he's going to borrow or rent the cabin often. It makes a wonderful weekend retreat. It's strange how he can always get off when he really feels he has to.

January 13

George asked me out for Friday night. He's kind of nothing but I guess that's the safest kind.

January 14

Lane met me during lunch and insisted that I get him a
new contact. His connection has been busted and he's
really hurting. He twisted my arm until it is black and
blue and made me promise I'd get him at least a lid for
tonight. I don't have any idea how to go about it. Chris
suggested I get it from Joe, but I don't want anything to
do with any of that bunch. I'm so scared I'm almost
sick, in fact I really am sick.

January 15

Dear unknowing Mother! Lane called twice last night
and insisted that he had to talk to me, but Mother sensed
that something was wrong and told him I was ill and
absolutely could not be disturbed. She's even encour-
aged me to stay home from school today – imagine
HER encouraging *me* to miss school when she's always
had such a big hang up about it. Anyway I do appreciate
that she cares and I just wish I could confide in her. I
wonder how much Lane really knows about Rich and
me? ? ? ? ?

January 17

George took me to the dance at school but it was all ruined because Joe and Lane were on my head all night. George wanted to know what was going on, so I told him that Lane was jealous because he had asked me out and I turned him down. Thank heavens the music was loud and we weren't able to do much talking. I wish they would leave me alone!

January 20

Dad will be all tied up next weekend so we won't be able to get away, but at least we can keep busy. Mom said she would help me make a new vinyl, leather-looking suit.

January 21

Gloria and Babs met me after school and walked part of the way home with me. I didn't know how to get rid of them without being completely hostile, but I wish they'd all get off my back. Mom drove by just as we got to the corner of Elm and I waved her down. It was too much! The entire drive home she kept saying what nice girls Gloria and Babs are and how good it would be for me to have many friends instead of just concentrating on Chris. Oh if she only knew, if she only knew!

January 24

Oh damn, damn, damn, it's happened again. I don't know whether to scream with glory or cover myself with ashes and sackcloth, whatever that means. Anyone who says pot and acid are not addicting is a damn, stupid, raving idiot, unenlightened fool! I've been on them since July 10, and when I've been off I've been scared to death to even think of anything that even looks or seems like dope. All the time pretending to myself that I could take it or leave it!

All the dumb, idiot kids who think they are only chipping are in reality just existing from one experience to the other. After you've had it, there isn't even life without drugs. It's a prodding, colorless, dissonant bare existence. It stinks. And I'm glad I'm back. Glad! Glad! Glad! I've never had it better than I had it last night. Each new time is the best time and Chris feels the same way. Last night when she called and asked me to come over, I knew something terrible had happened. She sounded like she didn't know what to do. But when I got there and smelled that incredible smell, I just sat down on the floor of her room with her and cried and smoked. It was beautiful and wonderful and we'd been without it for so long. I'll never be able to express how really great it is.

Later I called Mother and told her I was spending the night with Chris because she felt a little depressed. Depressed? No one in the world but a doper could know the true opposite of depressed.

January 26

Chris feels a little guilty but I'm delighted that we're turned on again, we belong to the world! The world belongs to us! Poor old George is going to have to go the way of all squares. He drove by to pick me up for school and I couldn't have been less interested. I don't even need him for a chauffeur anymore.

January 30

I talked to Lane today and he's really amazing. He's got a new connection and he can get me anything I want. So I told him I like uppers best. Who needs to go down when you can go up? Right?

February 6

Life is really unbelievable now. Time seems so endless yet everything goes so fast. I love it!

P.S. Mother's really glad that I'm 'in' again. She likes to hear the telephone ringing for me. Isn't that too much!

February 13

Lane was hit last night. I don't know how they found out about him but I guess he was pushing too much too fast to those little teeny boppers of his. I'm just grateful I wasn't there. Being so sweet and innocent and naive, my parents don't let me stay out late on week nights. They are trying to protect me from the big bad bogie man. I'm not really too worried about Lane. He's barely sixteen so they probably won't give him too much of a problem – probably slap his hands.

February 18

Our supply has dried up somewhat with Lane on good behavior, but Chris and I are very resourceful. Anyway we're managing.

I think I'm going to start taking the pill. It's a lot easier than worrying. I bet the pill is harder to get than drugs – which shows you how screwed up this world really is!

February 23

Dear Diary,

Oh, wow! They raided Chris's house last night while her folks and her aunt were out, but Chris and I played the game. The big blue badge just stood shaking his head while Chris and I swore to our parents it was our very first time and that nothing had really happened. Thank God they arrived while we still had our brains together. I wonder how they knew we were there? ? ? ?

February 24

This is the funniest thing I have ever heard: Mom is worried and hinting that something might have happened to her little baby in those words she can't bring herself to use. She wants me to go see Doctor Langley for a checkup, isn't that a laugh?

It took me a while to plead ignorance and innocence with my eyes opened as wide as they would go. I pretended I didn't even know what she was talking about, and do you know, she finally wound up actually feeling guilty for ever even suspecting such a thing.

(?)

We're all on probation, and are not supposed to see each other and Mom and Dad are sending me to a head-shrinker beginning next Monday. I guess that was all part of the bargain to keep me out of court. The rumor is that Lane has been sent away someplace, to a lock-in, dry-out school I think. Actually this was his third bust. I didn't know that. Well, at least he can't think I had anything to do with it since I too got caught up in the drag. At least this is my first charge. I guess actually I'm pretty lucky.

February 27

You'd think I was six years old the way Mom and Dad are watching me. I have to come straight home from school as if I were a baby. This morning when I left Mom's parting words were, 'Come straight home after school.' Wow! Like I'm going to get stoned at 3:30 – it doesn't sound so bad at that.

Later

After dinner I was going to walk down to the drugstore to get some colored pencils to finish my map and as I started out the door Mom called to Tim and told him to go with me. That is really too much! Having my little brother watching me! He didn't like the idea any better than I did. I almost felt like telling him why she wanted him to go with me! It would serve him right. It would serve them all right. I know what I ought to do, I ought to turn him on! Maybe I will! Maybe I'll surprise him with a trip on a piece of candy. Wow! I just wish I could be sure it would be a bummer.

March 1

I'm about to blow. This whole set-up is beginning to bug me until my nerves are all crawling. I can hardly even go to the bathroom by myself.

March 2

Today I went to the headshrinker's, a fat ugly little man who doesn't even have enough balls to lose weight. Man, I almost recommended some amphetamines – they'd cut his appetite and give him a blast at the same time. That's probably what he needs, sitting there peering over his glasses waiting for me to tell him some gory details. He's almost worse than anything else that's happened to me.

March 5

Jackie slipped me a couple of co-pilots in English when she passed out the test papers. Tonight after everyone goes to bed I'll get high all by myself. I can hardly wait!

(?) *

Like here I am in Denver. When I was high I just walked out and hitch-hiked here, but now it seems crazy quiet and unreal, maybe that's because it's still early. I hope so, I've only got the twenty dollars that I took from Dad's pants, but no source.

---

* There are no dates for the following material. It was recorded on single sheets of paper, paper bags, etc.

(?)

I'm sharing a place with a couple of kids I met, but they think it's kind of dull here so we're going to go to Oregon and see what's happening in Coos Bay. We've got enough acid to keep us all stoned for the next two weeks or forever, and that's all that counts.

March . . .

I haven't any clothes except these I had on when I left home and I'm getting so damned dirty I think they've grown on me. It was snowing in Denver, but it's so penetratingly damp here in Oregon it's a hell of a sight worse. I've got a fucking head cold and I feel miserable, and my period has started and I don't have any Tampax. Hell, I wish I had a shot.

(?)

Last night I slept in the park curled under a shrub and today it's drizzling and I can't find any of the kids I came from Denver with. Finally I went into a church and asked the janitor or whatever he was what I should do. He told me to sit here till it stopped raining, then go down to some kind of Salvation Army type place. I guess I have no choice since I know I've got a fever and I'm dripping wet and so filthy and smelly I can hardly stand myself. I'm trying to use some paper towels from the wash room for Kotex, and man that is some damned inconvenience. Oh, if I only had an upper.

This is a nice church. It's small and quiet and clean. I feel dreadfully out of place here, and I'm beginning to feel so damned lonely I've got to get out of here. Guess I'll try finding the mission or whatever the hell it is in the rain. I just hope I don't lose the bloody goddamned paper towels in the center of some street.

Later

This is really a great place! It really is! They let me have a shower and gave me some clean old square clothes and some Kotex and fed me even though I told them I wouldn't go by their hard stooled rules. They wanted me to stay here a few days and let them contact my parents to work out something so that we could bridge our differences. But my parents aren't about to let me use acid and pot and I'm not about to give them up! This guy was really nice. He is even driving me up to a health clinic to get something for my cold. I really feel lousy, maybe the good doctor will give me something to make me feel better, like wow! Anything! I wish the other old jerk would hurry up doing whatever he is doing so we could go.

It's still the . . . whatever it is. I met a girl, Doris, in the doctor's waiting room who said I could come share her pad since the couple she lived with and her boyfriend split during the night. Then the doc gave me a shot and a bottle of vitamins, imagine vitamins! He said my body is run down and malnourished, like that of most of the other kids he sees. He really was nice though. He just acted like he cared and told me to come back in a few days. I told him I didn't have any bread and he just laughed and said he'd have been surprised if I had.

(?)

At last the bitchin' rain has quit. Doris and I walked all through Coos Bay. They've really got some shops! I told her about the place Chris and I had opened and Doris wants to get a place when we get a few crumbs, but somehow it doesn't really seem very important anymore. Doris has a whole can of pot so we'll have joints for a long time. We were kind of stoned and everything seemed up even though my ass is still dragging.

It's good enough to just be alive. I love Coos Bay, and I love acid! The people here, at least here in our section of town, are beautiful. They understand life and they understand me. I can talk like I want and dress like I want and nobody cares. Looking at the posters in the store windows, and even walking around past the Greyhound bus station to watch who is coming in is groovy. We went by a place where they make posters and I'm going to help Doris cover the walls when we get a few crumbs together. We stopped at a Coffee House and the Digger Free Store and the Psychedelic Shop. Tomorrow we're going to see the rest of the sights. Doris has been here a couple of months and she knows everything and everybody. I was amazed when I found out that she was only fourteen. I thought she was a very small and immature eighteen or nineteen.

(?)

Last night Doris was really low. We've run out of pot and money and we're both hungry and the damnable rain has started puking up again. This little one room has only the one burner stove which doesn't seem to give out any heat at all. My ears and sinus cavities (see, I know, I watch TV, or used to) all feel like they've been poured full of concrete, and my chest must surely be bound with a steel band. We'd walk someplace and try to get a free meal or thug something but it's hardly worth the effort in the rain, so I guess we'll just eat noodles and dry cereal again. We've talked about how we hated the tourists and the phonies and the beggars here, but I think I'll go join the ranks tomorrow and try to beg enough bread for a little food and a fix. Doris and I really need both.

(?)

Oh, to be stoned, to have someone tie me off and give me a shot of anything. I've heard paregoric is great. Oh hell, I wish I had enough anything to end the whole shitty mess.

I've been asleep and I don't know if it's the same day or week or year, but who the hell cares anyway?

The goddamned rain is even worse than yesterday. It's like the whole sky is pissing on us. I tried to go out once, but my cold is so bad I was chilled to my ass before I'd even gotten to the goddamned corner, so I came back and went to bed with my clothes on, trying to curl up enough so my body heat would at least keep me from dying. I guess I've got a high fever, because I keep drifting off – that's the only beJesus thing that keeps me from croaking. Oh, I need a fix *so* bad! I want to scream and pound my head against the wall and climb the damned dusty, faded stringy curtains. I've got to get out of here. I've got to get the hell out of here before I really blow my cool all the way. I'm scared and lonely and I'm sick. I'm as sick as I've ever been in my life.

I tried not to let myself think of home till Doris got started on her screwing life's history, and now I'm really falling apart at the seams. God, if I had enough money I would go back where I came from or at least call. Tomorrow I'll go back to the church and ask them to call my folks. I don't know why I've acted like such an ass when I've always had it so good. Poor Doris has had nothing but shit since she was ten years old. Her mother was married four times by the time Doris was ten and had humped with who knows how many men in between. And when Doris had just turned eleven her current stepfather started having sex with her but good, and the poor little stupid bastard didn't even know what to do about it because he threatened to kill her if she ever told her mother or anyone else. So she put up with the sonofabitch balling her till she was twelve. Then one day when he had hurt her pretty bad she told her gym teacher why she couldn't do the exercises. The teacher had her taken away and put into a juvenile home till they could find a foster home. But even that wasn't much better, because both the teenage brothers gave it to her and later on an older teenage girl tuned her in and turned her on drugs, then took her the homo route. Since then she's pulled down her pants and hopped into bed with anyone who would turn down the covers, or part the bushes. Oh Father, I've got to get out of the cesspool! It's sucking me down and drowning me! I've got to get the hell out of here while I still can. Tomorrow! Tomorrow for sure! After the goddamned rain stops!

(?)

Who the hell cares? At last the goddamned rain has stopped! The sky is as blue as it was ever meant to be, which I gather is unusual for this area. Doris and I are both going to cut out of this asinine assed place. There's going to be a rally in Southern California. Wow! Here we come!

(?)

I'm actually and literally and completely sick to my stomach. I want to puke all over the shitty world. Most of the way down we rode with a big fat assed, baby screwing truck driver who picked us up and got his kicks by physically hurting Doris and watching her cry. When he stopped for gas we both sneaked out even though he had threatened us. Man, what a mother . . . We finally got another ride with some of our kind and while they shared their grass with us it must have been some home grown stuff, because it was so fuckin weak it could barely get us off terra firm.

(?)

The rally itself was great, acid and booze and pot as free as the air. Even now colors are still dripping down over me and the crack in the window is beautiful. This life is beautiful. It's so goddamned beautiful I can hardly stand it. And I'm a glorious part of it! Everybody else is just taking up space. Goddamned stupid people. I'd like to shove life down all their throats and then maybe they'd understand what it's all about.

Near the door a fat girl with long stringy blonde hair is getting to her knees on a green upon green upon purple robe. She's got a guy with her and he has a ring in his nose and multi-colored designs on his shaven head. They keep saying 'love' to each other. It's beautiful to watch. Color intermingled with color. People intermingled with people. Color and people intercoursing together.

(?)

I don't know what or when or where or who it is! I only know that I am now a Priestess of Satan trying to maintain after a freak-out to test how free everybody was and to take our vows.

Dear Diary,

I feel awfully bitched and pissed off at everybody. I'm really confused. I've been the digger here, but now when I face a girl it's like facing a boy. I get all excited and turned-on. I want to screw with the girl, you know, and then I get all tensed-up and scared. I feel goddamned good in a way and goddamned bad in a way. I want to get married and have a family, but I'm afraid. I'd rather be liked by a guy than a girl. I'd rather screw with a guy, but I can't. I guess I've had a bit of a bummer. Sometimes I want one of the girls to kiss me. I want her to touch me, to have her sleep under me, but then I feel terrible. I get guilty and it makes me sick. Then I think of my mother. I think of screaming at her and telling her to make room for me because I'm coming home and I feel like a man. Then I get sick and I just want anybody and I should be out doing my digging. I'm really sick. I'm really way out of it.

Dear Diary,

It's a thousand light years later, lunar time.

Everybody's been storytelling except me. I don't have any stories worth telling. All I can do is draw pictures of monsters and internal organs and hate.

(?)

Another day, another blow job. The fuzz has clamped down till the town is mother dry. If I don't give Big Ass a blow he'll cut off my supply. Hell, I'm shaking on the inside more than I'm shaking on the outside. What a bastard world without drugs! The dirty ofay who wants me to lay it on him knows my ass is dragging, but he's doling out the only supply I know about. I'm almost ready to take on the Fat Cats, the Rich Philistines, or even the whole public for one good shot. Goddamn Big Ass makes me do it before he gives me the load. Everybody is just lying around here like they're dead and Little Jacon is yelling, 'Mama, Daddy can't come now. He's humping Carla.' I've got to get out of this shit hole.

(?)

I don't know what the hell hour or day or even year it is, or even what town. I guess I've had a blackout or they've been passing some bad pills. The girl on the grass beside me is white-faced and Mona Lisa like and she's preggers. I asked her what she was going to do with the baby and she just said, 'It will belong to everybody. We'll all share her.'

I wanted to go and find someone who's holding, but the baby thing really bugged me. So I asked her for an upper and she just shook her head like a stupid, blank, and I realized that she's completely burned out. Behind that beautiful stoned face is a big dried-up bunch of ashes and she's lying there like a stupid dumb shit who can't do anything.

Well, at least I'm not burned out and I'm not preg. Or maybe I am. I couldn't take the goddamn pill even if I had it. No doper can take the pill because they don't know what the hell day it is. So maybe I am pregnant. So what. There's a pre-med drop-out wandering around somewhere who will take care of it. Or maybe some goddamn prick would stomp on me during a freak out and I'd lose it anyway. Or maybe the sonofabitch bomb will go off tomorrow. Who knows?

When I look around here at all the ass draggers, I really think that we are a bunch of gutless wonders. We get pissed off when someone tells us what to do, but we don't know what to do unless some fat bastard tells us. Let somebody else think for us and do for us and act for us. Let them build the roads and the cars and the houses, run the lights and the gas and the water and the sewers. We'll just sit here on our blistered tails with our minds exploding and our hands out. God, I sound like a goddamn Establishmentarian, and I haven't even got a pill to take the taste out of my mouth or drive the bullshit thoughts away.

When?

A raindrop just splashed on my forehead and it was like a tear from heaven. Are the clouds and the skies really weeping over me? Am I really alone in the whole wide gray world? Is it possible that even God is crying for me? Oh no . . . no . . . no . . . I'm losing my mind. Please God, help me.

(?)

I gather from the sky that it is early morning. I've been reading a paper that the wind blew up beside me. It says one girl had her baby in the park, another had a miscarriage and two unidentified boys died during the night from O.D.'s. Oh, how I wish one of them had been me!

Another day

I finally talked to an old priest who really understands young people. We had an endlessly long talk about why young people leave home, then he called my Mom and Dad. While I waited for him to get the call through I looked at myself in the mirror. I can't believe that I have changed so little. I expected to look old and hollow and gray, but I guess it's only me on the inside that has shriveled and deteriorated. Mom answered the phone in the family room, and Dad ran upstairs to get the extension, and the three of us almost drowned out the connection. I can't understand how they can possibly still love me and still want me but they do! They do! They do! They were glad to hear from me and to know I am all right. And there were no recriminations or scoldings or lectures or anything. It's strange that when something happens to me Dad always leaves everything in the whole world and comes. I think if he were on a peace mission involving all humanity in all the galaxies he would leave to come to me. He loves me! He loves me! He loves me! He truly does! I just wish I could love myself. I don't know how I can treat my family like I have. But I'm going to make it all up to them, I'm through with all the shit. I'm not even going to talk about it or write about it or even think about it any-more. I am going to spend the rest of my entire life trying to please them.

Dear Diary,

I couldn't sleep, so I've been wandering the streets. I look kind of square because I don't want to seem weird when my parents get here. I've got my hair tied back in a ponytail and I traded clothes with the most conservative girl I could find, and I'm wearing an old pair of white tennies I found in the gutter. At first the kids I talked to in the coffee house seemed a little uptight because of the way I looked, but when I told them I'd called my folks to come and get me they all seemed glad.

It seems inconceivable that all the time Chris and I were in Berkeley we didn't find out anything about any of the kids. It was just one big tearing down everything and everybody vacuum. Tonight I learned about Mike and Marie and Heidi and Lilac and many others. I'll probably use up the rest of the pages writing about them, but that's good because I want to get a fresh new clean book when I get home. You, dear Diary, will be my past. The one I will buy when we get home will buy my future. So now I must hurry and write about the people I have met just this night. It simply amazes me that so many parents and kids have trouble over their hair! My parents were always bugging me about mine. They wanted me to curl it or cut it or get it out of my eyes, or tie it back etc., etc., etc. Sometimes I think that was our biggest bone of contention. I met Mike at the coffee house, and after explaining my situation and my current curiosity about why kids run away he became very communicative and told me that *hair* had been one of his problems too. In fact his dad had become so angry that twice he had forcibly shaved his head and sideburns. Mike said his parents were taking away all his freedom and power of decision. He was becoming dehumanized, mechanized, forced into the mold of his father. He was not even allowed to decide which classes he wanted to take in school! He said he wanted art, but his parents thought only weaklings and bums were artists. Finally he ran away to preserve his personality and sanity. So I told Mike about the church and their efforts to bring about a new and human arrangement between my parents and me. I hope he goes there.

Then I talked to Alice, who I met just sitting stoned on the curb. She didn't know whether she was running away from something or running to something, but she admitted that deep in her heart she wanted to go home.

The others I talked to, the ones who had homes, all seemed to want to go back, but felt they couldn't because that would mean giving up their identity. It made me think about the hundreds of thousands of kids who have run away and are wandering around all over the place. Where do they come from? Where do they even manage to crash for the night? Most of them don't have any money and don't have anywhere to go.

I think I'll go into child guidance when I get out of school. Or maybe I should become a psychologist. At least I'd be able to understand where kids are at and maybe that would help compensate for what I've done to my family and myself. Perhaps it was even right for me to go through all this suffering so that I could be more understanding and tolerant of the rest of humanity.

Oh dear wonderful, trusting, friendly Diary, that's exactly what I'll do. I'll spend the rest of my life helping people who are just like me! I feel so good and happy. I finally have something to do for the rest of my life. Wow! I'm through with drugs too. I've used the hard stuff only a few times and I don't like it. I don't like any of it. The uppers or the downers. I'm through with the whole mess. Absolutely and completely and forever, really I am.

Later
I have just read the stuff I wrote in the last few weeks and I am being drowned in my own tears, suffocated, submerged, inundated, overpowered. They are a lie! A bitter, evil cursed lie! I could never have written things like that! I could never have done things like that! It was another person, someone else! It must have been! It had to be! Someone evil and foul and degenerate wrote in my book, took over my life. Yes, they did, they did! But even as I write I know I am telling even a bigger lie! Or am I? Has my mind been damaged? Was it really just a nightmare and it seems real? I think I've mixed up things which are true and things which are not. All of it couldn't be true. I must be insane.

I have lamented until I am dehydrated, but calling myself a wretched fool, a beggarly, worthless, miserable, paltry, mean, pitiful, unfortunate, woebegone, tormented, afflicted, shabby, disreputable, deplorable human being isn't going to help me either. I have two choices; I must either commit suicide or try to rectify my life by helping others. That is the path I must take, for I cannot bring further disgrace and suffering upon my family. There is nothing more to say, dear Diary, except I love you, and I love life and I love God. Oh I do. I really do.

DIARY NUMBER TWO

April 6

What a wonderful time to start a new diary and a new life. It is spring. I am home again with my family. Gran and Gramps will be here for another reunion with the prodigal daughter. Tim and Alexandria are just themselves, and nothing could be better! I don't remember who wrote 'God is in His Heaven and all's right with the world,' but that is exactly the way I feel.

Anyone who has desperately needed to come home knows what a tremendous feeling it is to be lying in his own bed! My pillow! My mattress! My old silver hand mirror. It all seems so permanent, so old and new at the same time. But I wonder if I will ever feel completely new again. Or will I spend the rest of my life feeling like a walking disease? ? ? ?

When I go into counseling I'm really going to try to

make kids see that getting into drugs simply isn't worth the bullshit! Sure, it's great and groovy going on trips, I will never be able to say it isn't. It's exciting and colorful and dangerous, but it isn't worth it! It simply isn't worth it! Every day for the rest of my life I shall dread weakening again and becoming something I simply do not want to be! I'll have to fight it every day of my life and I hope God will help me. I hope I haven't ruined everyone's life by coming home. I hope Tim and Alex wouldn't be better off if I'd stayed away.

April 7

Today Tim and I took a long walk through the park. I talked to him honestly about drugs, after all he's thirteen and knows kids who use pot at school. Of course I didn't tell him the details about my past, but we did discuss the important things in life like religion and God and our parents and the future and the war and all the things that kids talk about when they're stoned. It was different and really beautiful. Tim has such a clear, decent, honorable outlook on life. I'm glad he's my brother. I'm proud he's my brother! I'm grateful that he will be seen with me. I'm sure it's embarrassing to him, because everyone knows I was busted and that I ran away. Boy, have I ever messed up my life! Tim and I can communicate and he says he can pretty well bridge the gap with Mom and Dad. He is very tolerant about their position as parents and tries to see things from their point of view. He is really a very special person. I wonder how much of his mature outlook I am responsible for? I know he must have done a lot of thinking while I was missing and Mom and Dad were losing their minds with worry and fear and anxiety. Crap, what an idiot I have been.

April 8

Today Gran and Gramps arrived. We went to the airport to meet them and I cried like a big boob. They seem to have aged so much and I know I am responsible for much of it. Gramps is completely gray and Gran's face is lined with deep furrows that weren't there the last time I saw her. Could I have done all that in a month! In the car on the way home Gramps scratched my back like he used to do when I was a little girl and whispered to me that I had only to forgive myself. He's such a nice man and I shall really try, although I know it won't be easy. I must try to make them proud of me again.

Later

I couldn't sleep, so I got up and took a walk around the house. Alex's mother cat just had a batch of baby kittens and I sat on the porch and just kept looking at them. It was a revelation! Without drugs! Without anything but kittens whose fur is like all the softness in the world put together. It was so soft that when I closed my eyes I wasn't sure I was even touching it. I put the little gray one, named Happiness, up to my ear, and felt the warmth in her tiny body and listened to her incredible purring. Then she tried to nurse my ear and the feeling in me was so big I thought I was going to break wide open. It was better than a drug trip, a thousand times better, a million times, a trillion times. These things are real! The softness was not a hallucination; the sounds of the night, the cars swishing by, the crickets. I was really there. I heard it! I saw it and I felt it and that's the way I want life to always be! And that's the way it will be!

April 9

Today I went back to school and was called into the principal's office immediately. He informed me that he had a record of my behavior and that I was a disgusting example of young American womanhood. Then he told me that I was thoroughly selfish, undisciplined and immature and that he would not tolerate any misbehavior on my part at all. Then he sent me to my classes like garbage thrown in a disposal. What a jerk!

If I ever had any doubts about going into psychiatric work and guidance work, I don't have them now. Kids need understanding, listening, caring individuals. They need me! The coming generation needs me! And that poor stupid, idiot man who has probably run hundreds of kids out of school has given me a personal challenge. He may drive other kids away, but not me! I studied for four hours tonight and I'm going to study my stupid head off until I'm completely caught up. Even if it takes me seven or eight hours a night!

See ya.

April 10

Now that I have a goal I feel a lot stronger myself. In fact I'm feeling stronger every day. Maybe I can really resist drugs now, instead of just conning myself like I did before.

April 11

Dear Diary,

I don't want to write this down because I really want to blot it out of my mind forever, but I'm so terrified that maybe if I tell you, it won't seem so terrible. Oh Diary, please help me. I'm scared. I'm so scared that my hands are sticky and I'm actually shaking.

I guess I must have had a flashback because I was sitting on my bed planning my mother's birthday, just thinking about what to get her and how to make it a surprise, when my mind got all mixed up. I can't really explain it, but it seemed to be rolling backwards, like it was rolling in on itself, and there was nothing I could do to stop it. The room got smoky and I thought I was in a head shop. We were all standing around reading the ads for the second-hand junk and for every kind of sex deal imaginable. And I started to laugh. I felt great! I was the highest person in the world and I was looking down at everyone and the whole world was in strange angles and shadows.

Then suddenly it all changed into some kind of underground movie. It was slow and lazy and the lighting was really weird. Naked girls were dancing around, making love to statues. I remember one girl ran her tongue along a statue and he came alive and took her off into the high, blue grass. I couldn't really see what was happening, but he was obviously putting it to her. I felt so sexy I wanted to break wide open and run after them. But the next thing I remember, I was back on the street, panhandling, and we were all shouting at the tourists, 'Mighty kind of y'all. I hope you have a nice orgasm with your dog tonight.'

Then I felt like I was being smothered and I was up in a glare of revolving lights and beacons. Everything was going around. I was a shooting star, a comet piercing the firmament, blazing through the sky. When I finally got myself together, I was lying on the floor nude.

I still can't believe it. What's happening to me? I was just lying on my bed, planning my mother's birthday, listening to records and bham!

Maybe it wasn't a flashback. Maybe I'm schizo. That often starts in teenagers when they lose contact with reality, doesn't it? Whatever it is, I'm really screwed up. I can't even control my mind. The words I wrote when I was out are just squirming little lines and roads with a lot of rotten crap and symbols in between. Oh, what am I going to do? I need someone to talk to. I really and truly and desperately do. Oh God, please help me. I'm so scared and so cold and so alone. I have only you, Diary. You and me, what a pair.

Later

I've done a few problems in math and even read a few pages. At least I can still read. I memorized a few lines and my mind seems to be functioning pretty well now. I did exercises too and I guess I've got control of my body. But I wish I had someone to talk to, someone who knows what's happening and what will happen. But I don't, so I must forget this thing. Forget, forget, forget, and not look back. I'll go ahead with Mom's party. Maybe I can get Tim and Alex to take her to an early movie after school and then I can have a lovely dinner ready on the table when they get home. I'll pretend this has all been a nightmare and forget it. Please God, let me forget it and don't let it happen again. Please, please, please.

April 12

I kept very busy today and I didn't think about it once. I think I'll set my hair the way Mom likes it for tomorrow. That should make her happy.

April 13

It was a lovely birthday. Tim and Alex took Mom to see an early movie, which I think she liked even more than they did. Dad had to work late at his office and I was glad because I would have felt terribly self-conscious with him in the kitchen and me not knowing what I was doing, but everything just turned out beautifully. The chicken looked like *Better Homes and Gardens*'s, only better, because it smelled good too, and the asparagus was nice and tender and the rolls were just exactly like Gran would have made. In fact, I wish she had been here, she would have been proud of me. We had a fresh fruit cup and wilted lettuce salad with bacon dressing, it was a little too wilted, in fact much too wilted, but everyone pretended they didn't notice and Daddy teased me and said he wouldn't be surprised if I didn't make some young man a good wife someday. I hope he didn't notice the tears in my eyes, because I so much want to do just that!

For dessert we just had fresh peach ice cream with frozen peaches over it and the whole thing was really pretty great, particularly since it was the first complete meal I ever cooked by myself. Alex made Mom a little ceramic candy dish shaped like her hand. It is really lovely, and all the more lovely because, with the help of only her Girl

Scout teacher, she had it fired and everything without Mom even knowing. I used to be kind of jealous of Alex and I guess had a lot of hostility toward her even though I loved her. But now things are different. I really feel something new and wonderful and exciting is beginning to grow within me. Maybe that's the way people get extra love to cover every child that's born?

Oh, I do hope that someday someone will want to marry me.

April 14

I got up really early this morning so I could take a long leisurely bath before Tim and Alex start pounding on the bathroom door. It was great. I love taking my time and enjoying life. After I shaved my legs and underarms, I really looked at my body critically for the first time in my life. It's a nice body but a little small through the bust. I wonder what would happen if I exercised. But then, I guess I'm afraid that I'd wind up looking like a jersey cow. I'm glad I'm a girl. I even like having my periods. I guess I never wanted to be a boy. A lot of girls do wish they were boys, but not me. It's hard to believe that at one point I was so screwed up I didn't know what I was. Oh, I wish I could wipe away all that rotten past. I know Gramps is right. I must forgive and forget but I just can't. I simply can't! When I'm having the very nicest thoughts, the black ugly past comes flooding in like a nightmare. And it's ruined my whole day already.

(?)

Guess what? Your genius friend got everything right on her English exam today. I know I did because it was so easy and I think I did almost as well in math. I might have missed two or three, but I know it couldn't have been more than that. Isn't that exciting?

April 19

Cripes! It's started again! I met Jan downtown and she asked me to a 'party' tonight. None of the kids think I'm really going to stay off, because most of those who've been busted before are just being more careful and discreet. When I told Jan, 'No, thanks,' she just smiled! It scared me to death. She didn't say anything at all. She just smiled at me like, 'We know you'll be back.' Oh, I hope not. I really hope not.

April 21

George just says 'hi' to me in the coldest way. It's completely obvious that he's really straight and doesn't want
to be connected in any way with a doper. All the kids at
school pretty much know who's on and who's off and I
want to get in with the square kids, but I don't see how
I'm going to do it with my reputation hanging over me.
I couldn't tell Mom and Dad this, but I really would like
to go out on dates. I don't mean with the grass gang, but
with the nice kids. I'd like to have a boy put his arm
around me in a movie. But how could I ever have that
with one of the heads? Everyone knows that sex and
shit* go together, and as far as I'm concerned they are a
bunch of social lepers – and that's the way the straight
kids feel too.

The only sad thing is that I'm still classed as one of
them, and I guess I always will be! It's strange how much
sex I've had and yet I don't feel as though I've had any. I
still want somebody to be nice and just kiss me goodnight at the door. That's a laugh! Oh Diary, forgive me. I
am trying so hard to have a positive outlook, but I can't.
I can't. You're the only one I can really open my soul to. I

---

* drugs

want to go back and blot out everything and start over. But inside I'm old and hard and I'm probably responsible for I don't know how many junior high and grade school kids getting hung up, and they probably have turned around and hung up other kids. How can God ever forgive me? Why would He want to?

I guess I'd better go take a bath before my parents hear these stupid-assed, crazy sobs which I can no longer control.

Thanks for listening.

April 24

The kids have really started hassling me. Twice today Jan banged into me in the hall and called me Nancy Nice and Mary Pure. But I've had it. I really have had it this time and if I begin to feel too low, I'm just going to ask Mom and Dad to transfer me to another school. But the problem is where could I go that somebody would not find out about me? And how could I tell Mom and Dad everything so they'd let me change schools? Oh, I really don't know what I'm going to do. I've even started praying every night like I used to when I was little, but now I'm not just saying words, I'm begging. I'm pleading.

Goodnight Diary.

April 27

It's terrible not to have a friend. I'm so lonely and so alone. I think it's worse on weekends than during the week, but I don't know. It's pretty bad all the time.

April 28

I got some papers back today and I haven't gotten anything under a B+. I'm also starting a file of statistics relating to kids and drugs. Someday I'll tell you about it when I don't have to spend every minute studying.

May 1

Gramps had a stroke. It happened during the night, and Mom and Dad are flying out there today. They'll be gone when we get home from school. They are so sweet. They were more worried about leaving me than anything else. I'm sure they know how lonely and frustrated I am and I'm sure they ache inside as I do about Gramps. I used to think I was the only one who felt things. but I really am only one infinitely small part of an aching humanity. It's a good thing most people bleed on the inside or this would really be a gory, blood-smeared earth.

Gran will be so lonely if Gramps dies. I just can't picture her without him. It would be like cutting a full person in half. Sweet old Gramps, he used to call me his Five-Star General. I think I'll write to him before I leave for school and sign it 'Gramps' Five-Star General.' No one else will know what I'm talking about, but he'll know.

Bye now.

(?)

Dad just called to see if we were all right and to tell us Gramps is worse. He's in a coma now and all of us are pretty upset, particularly Alex. When I tucked her in bed like Mom always does and kissed her goodnight, she asked if she could come and get into bed with me if she got scared during the night. Sweet little thing. But what do you say to someone when they feel rotten and there are no answers? ? ?

Then I went into Tim's room and kissed him goodnight. He's pretty upset too and I guess we're all in rotten shape, even Dad.

May 4

Tim and Alex and I all got up at the same time and straightened our rooms and fixed our cereal and fruit and cleaned up the dishes together. We were really quite efficient, if you can believe that!

Gotta go to school but I'll write more tonight if anything great or tragic happens.

9:50 P.M.
Dad called, but things are about the same. Gramps is a little worse but still holding on. They can't really tell which way he is going to go. I guess he's pretty critical though. Alex clung to me and cried. I feel like crying myself. The house seems so big and lonely and quiet without Mom and Dad.

May 5

Gramps died during the night. The day after tomorrow Doctor ——— from the university is going to take Tim and Alex and me to the airport and we'll fly to his funeral. It seems unbelievable that I will never see

Gramps again. I wonder what has happened to him. I hope he's not just cold and dead. I can't bring myself to think of Gramps' body being eaten by worms and maggots. I just can't bear to think that. Maybe the embalming fluid they use just causes the body to disintegrate into dust. Oh, I surely hope so.

May 8

I couldn't believe *that* was Gramps lying in the casket. It was just a tired, drained skeleton covered by skin. Oh, I've seen dead frogs and birds and lizards and Easter chickens, but this was such a shock! It seemed unreal. It was almost like a bad trip. I'm so grateful I never had a bummer. But maybe if my first trip had been, I wouldn't have taken any more. In that respect I wish it had. Gran seemed so calm and loving. She had one arm around my shoulder and one around Alexandria's. Precious, strong Gran, even during the long, long, long, long, long funeral she didn't cry. She just sat there with her head bowed. It was a strange almost eerie thing but I felt as though Gramps was there beside her. I talked to Tim about it later and he felt exactly the same way.

When they lowered Gramps' body into the ground,

that was the worst part. That was positively the worst part in the whole world. Alexandria and I cried even though none of the rest of the family did. I tried to be as strong and controlled as they are, but I just simply couldn't. Mom and Gran and Dad dabbed at their eyes occasionally and Tim kept sniffing, and of course Alex is a little girl, but me, well, naturally I made a spectacle of myself again!

May 9

Gran is going home with us tonight and she'll stay till school is out. Then I'll come back with her and help her get organized to move in with us until she can find a little apartment close by.

I don't know when I have ever been so tired in my life. I can't even imagine how Gran holds up because I can barely move. All of us look as though we have been endlessly ill. Even little Alex is dragging. I wonder how long it will take us to adjust to life without Gramps? Will we ever be the same? How will dear, precious Gran manage? When she gets into her new apartment I'm going to stay with her often and take her to movies and go on long walks with her and things.

May 12

This morning I looked out the window and saw new green popping through the soil and I started crying uncontrollably again. I don't really understand the resurrection. I can't even conceive how Gramps' body which will decay and sour and mold and mildew and fall into crumbling little bits can ever come back together again. But I can't understand how a brown dried-up, shriveled little gladiola bulb can re-blossom either. I guess that God can put atoms and molecules and bodies together again if a gladiola bulb without even a brain can do it. This really makes me feel a lot better, and I don't know how I could ever expect to understand death when I can't even understand television or electricity, or even stereo for that matter. In fact I understand so little I don't know how I even exist.

I once read somewhere that man uses less than a tenth (I think) of his brain capacity. Imagine having 90% more thinking ability, and using every bit of it. That would be simply glorious! Imagine what a perfectly marvelous planet this would be if minds were 90 times more efficient than they are now?

May 14

I had a nightmare last night about Gramps' body all filled with maggots and worms, and I thought about what would happen if I should die. Worms don't make distinction under the ground. They wouldn't care that I'm young and that my flesh is solid and firm. Thank goodness Mom heard me moaning and came in and helped me get hold of myself. Then we went and got some hot milk, but I was still crawling and I couldn't tell her what had happened. I'm sure she thought it had something to do with the times I ran away, but I couldn't tell her because this was even more horrible.

I was still shivering after the milk, so we both put on shoes and walked around the yard. It was chilly even with our robes over our night clothes, but we talked about a lot of things including my becoming a social worker or something in that area, and Mom is very pleased that I want to help other people. She is really very understanding. Everybody should be as lucky as I am.

May 15

I have to force myself to concentrate in school. I didn't know that death took so much out of people. I feel completely drained still and have to force myself into everything I do.

May 16

Today Dad took me to an anti-war rally at the university. He is very worried and upset about the students and talked to me as though I were an adult. I really enjoyed it. Daddy is not as worried about the militant students (who he thinks should be dealt with very harshly) as he is about the kids who could be easily led into wrong thinking. I'm worried about them too. I'm worried about me!

Later we went over to see Doctor _____ who is also really concerned about the younger generation. He talked a lot about where kids are going and then he rattled off some statistics that really surprised me. I can't remember half of what he said he talked so fast, but there were things like: 1,000 college-age kids commit suicide every year and another 9,000 try to. VD has gone up 25% among kids my age and pregnancies are really growing, even with the pill. He also said that crime and mental illness among kids has skyrocketed. In fact, everything he said was worse than the thing before it.

When we left I don't know whether I felt better about what I've done because so many other people are caught up in the same thing or worse because everybody's going crazy at once. But to tell you the truth, I really don't think the kids can be blamed for screwing up, at least not entirely. The adults don't seem to be doing much better. In fact, I can't think of one person I'd like to see as President except Dad who'd never get elected with me for a daughter.

May 19

Well, I got blasted out of the water again today. Someone put a joint in my purse and I was so scared. I had to cut my next class and take a cab over to Dad's office.

I just don't understand why they won't leave me alone! Why are they hassling me like this? Does my existence make them nervous? I really think it does. I really think they are trying to wipe me off the face of the earth or send me to the nut house. It's like I've uncovered a giant spy ring and I can't be allowed to live anymore!

Dad said I have to be strong and adult. He talked to me for a long time and I'm really grateful that he cares, but I know he doesn't understand their motivations any better than I do. Besides he doesn't know about Richie and Lane and all the rest. He said the whole family is behind me. But what good does that do when the whole world is against me? It's like Gramps' dying. Everybody feels really terrible about it, but nobody can do anything, including me!

May 20

I've managed to get myself into the study grind again, which helps. At least it keeps my mind off you know what.

May 21

Gran is sick, but Mom thinks it's just the letdown. I hope so, because she really looks terrible. Oh, I almost forgot. Dad has gotten permission for me to use the university library, and today I went over for the first time. It's really fun. I felt very sophisticated and a lot of the kids think I'm a coed. Isn't that funny?

May 22

I met a boy in the library today. His name is Joel Reems and he's a freshman. We studied together, then he walked me over to Daddy's office. Daddy was busy, so we sat on the front steps of his building and waited for him. I decided to not pretend to Joel, but just to tell the truth about myself and let him take it or leave it (well, almost all the truth). I told him I was only sixteen and just had library privileges because of my Dad.

He's really a very sweet guy, because he just laughed and said that it was all right because he hadn't planned to ask me to marry him this semester anyway. When Dad came out, he sat on the steps for a while and the three of us talked like we had known each other always. It was great! Before Joel left he asked me when I'd be studying again and I said that I spent my entire waking hours studying, which seemed to please him.

May 23

Dear Daddy, I guess I should be mad at him but I'm not! He went and looked up Joel's record and told me all about him. I really got a kick out of the idea of Dad sneaking around the files getting information for me. Anyway Joel is an accelerated student who is in the university though he's only eighteen years old, barely. His dad is dead and his mother works in a factory and he works a seven-hour shift every day at the school as a janitor. He works from midnight till seven every morning, then his first class is at nine on Monday, Wednesday, and Friday. What a schedule! ! !

Dad warned me not to interfere with his studies, and I said I wouldn't. However if he wants to walk me from the library to Dad's office every afternoon (even Saturdays) I can't see what that could hurt, can you?

Evening

Joel did walk me to Dad's office. And it was almost like a date! Our words scrambled out all over each other and we laughed and chattered both at the same time. (It was very chaotic and very lovely.) Joel says he's never had much time for girls and he doesn't understand how I seem to know so much about him. I told him that women were very perceptive, that's all. And crafty!

May 25

Joel walked me over to Dad's office again tonight and it wasn't my idea but, Dad invited him over for dinner tomorrow. Mother said it's fine with her, and I know she's anxious to meet him because Daddy has been teasing me about him.

May 26

I raced home from school and helped Mom clean the house like the King of the World was coming, and I made sure we had all the ingredients for orange yeast rolls, my one specialty. I can't wait! I can't wait!

Later

Joel just left and it was a fantastic evening. I don't know why I say that because he and Daddy spent most of the time together. I guess it's because his dad died when he was seven, but they really had a nice relationship. Even Tim seemed fascinated while they talked, particularly about Joel's educational possibilities. (I think Tim is starting to think about college. Already!)

My orange rolls were perfection, even Gran said she couldn't have made better, and Joel ate seven! Seven! And he said he'd have taken a pocketful home for breakfast if there had been any left over. Of course if there had been any left over I'm sure he wouldn't have mentioned it. He's pretty reserved. I think I'll ask Mom if I can make him a batch and have him pick them up at Dad's office.

May 29

Oh Diary, guess what? Dad had absolutely the most wonderful news to tell us at dinner! (And he did it very nonchalantly.) He's going to try to get Joel a scholarship. He says he's pretty sure he can do it, but it will take time and he doesn't want me to say anything until it's all settled. I hope I can keep my big mouth shut. I'm not very good at that kind of thing.

P.S. Things seem okay at school. Nobody's talking to me, but nobody's hassling me either. I guess you can't have everything.

June 1

Gran's house was sold today and they've decided just to have the movers pack all her things and put them in storage. She broke down and cried when she heard the news. It's the first time I've really seen her cry. I guess Gramps' being gone and now the house which she lived in almost all her life, makes everything seem so final.

Later

I wonder if Joel really likes me? I wonder if he thinks I'm cute or pretty or attractive? I wonder if I seem like the kind of girl who would mean something serious to him? I hope he likes me because I like him a lot. In fact, I think I really love him . . .

Mrs Joel Reems

MRS JOEL REEMS

Mr and Mrs Joel Reems

Dr and Mrs Joel Reems

Doesn't that look lovely!

June 2

Mrs Larsen just called and said that Jan had promised to baby-sit but she called at the last minute and cancelled, which sounds just like Jan. Oh well, I guess I can study there as well as I can here. Gotta pack my things together.

See ya later.

P.M.

Dear Diary,

I'm really dragged and tired and sad and worn out and fed up.

Jan came by about a half an hour after Mrs Larsen left and said she wanted to baby-sit because she needed the bread. But I couldn't let her because she was stoned and Mrs Larsen's baby is only four months old. But she wouldn't leave so finally I had to call her parents and ask them to come and get her. I told them she was sick, but by the time they got there she was really grooving. She had the stereo on loud enough to wake the baby who was wet and crying anyway, but I didn't dare even change her because I wasn't sure what Jan might do. She was so high her mom and dad had to practically pull her out to the car, and they were both crying and asking me not to tell her parole officer.

Oh, I hope I did the right thing. I probably shouldn't have called her parents, but I really couldn't get her out of there and I surely couldn't have left her with the baby. I can just imagine what it's going to be like in school tomorrow when this gets around. Bahm! Nobody's even going to listen to my side. And besides, dopers don't understand things like hurting babies. They don't understand anything.

June 3

Mom and Dad said I did exactly as I should have last night and they were sorry they had not been available to help me. But what could they have done besides call Jan's parents? Actually it might have been even worse if they'd been there. Who knows? Gotta go now.

P.M.

Jan passed me in the hall today and there was bitterness and hostility in her face like I have never seen before. 'I'll get even with you, you fucking Miss Polly Pure,' she said and she practically screamed it out in front of everyone. I tried to explain but she turned and walked away as though I didn't even exist.

Later I went to the library. Joel knew something was wrong, so finally I told him I'm coming down with a cold and feel miserable. (The feeling miserable part is true.) He said I should take some aspirin and get some rest. Life is so simple for straight people.

(?)

I don't know what Jan has told all the kids, but she really must be starting some ugly rumors because now I get sneers and giggles which is worse than being lonely and ignored. I wish I could talk to Joel, but I'm not even going to the library to study I'm so uptight. I'll just take some books home and work in my room. (My room will be my whole universe.)

(?)

Joel just called from the library because he was worried about me. He had talked to Dad's secretary who didn't know anything. I'm so glad he called, but I told him I was sick and wouldn't be going to the library this week. (Oh, I am sick, I'm sick of the screwed-up potheads and acidheads and all the other dopey dopers who are persecuting me.) Anyway, Joel asked if I'd mind if he called me every night, and I didn't tell him that I'd be waiting by the phone but I will be! But you knew that didn't you?

June 7

During the night Gran got quite sick. I think she just doesn't care to go on without Gramps. She didn't come out of her room for breakfast. I took her a tray, but she just played around with the food. Tonight I must go in and visit with her instead of going to the library like I'd finally decided to do. Joel will understand.

Bye now.

June 8

I am so boxed in I don't know what to do. Jan sidled up to me as I was walking down the ramp and whispered, 'You better tell your little tail-wagging sister not to accept candy from strangers or even from friends, especially *your* friends.' But Jan wouldn't do that! She couldn't! No matter what she thinks of me she surely wouldn't take it out on Alexandria, would she? Would she? I wish I could make her understand, but I simply don't know how.

Oh, I would like to talk to Mom or Dad or Joel or Tim about this, but everything I do seems to make things worse. I guess I'll just have to work it into a dinner conversation some way about vindictive kids who put acid on candy and gum, etc., and pass them out. Maybe if I tell them that a teacher was talking about a kid in Detroit who died that way, they'll be careful. They've got to be careful!

June 9

I was walking home from the store and a carload of kids pulled up beside me and began shouting things like:

'Well, if it isn't easy lay, Mary Pure.'

'No, it's Miss Fink Mouth.'

'Miss Super Fink Mouth. Miss Double Triple Fink Mouth.'

'I wonder what would happen if we stashed some shit in her old man's car?'

'Wouldn't that be great having her father, the professor, picked up?'

Then they called me every rotten name in the book and roared off laughing hysterically, leaving me emotionally crushed and battered and beaten. I think they're just threatening me, trying to drive me crazy. But who knows? Last summer I read about some stoned kids who put a cat in a washing machine and turned it on just to see what would happen. Maybe they really would like to know how Dad would react. They're such a bunch of lousy crazy bastards I wouldn't put it past them. But I don't think they'll go that far. Maybe if I just sort of ignore them they will eventually give up.

June 10

For the first time I feel absolutely certain that even if I were locked in a room full of acid, Speed, and every other upper in the world I would only be disgusted, for

I see what it does to kids who used to be my friends. Surely they wouldn't pick on me so unmercifully if it weren't for drugs. Would they?

Today someone put a burning roach in my locker and when the principal called me out of my room even he knew I wouldn't do anything that stupid. My new jacket has a big hole in it and some loose papers had caught on fire and smoked everything all up. He asked me to name anyone I thought might have done it, and although I suspect Jan, I wouldn't dare tell on her, and I certainly don't want to name all the dopers at school. I'd be a fine one to point fingers. Besides they'd probably kill me. I'm really afraid.

June 11

I'm so grateful school will be out soon and next year maybe I can go to school in Seattle and live with Aunt Jeannie and Uncle Arthur. I do wish Gran hadn't sold her house, but sick as she is I guess I couldn't have lived there either.

P.S. I went to the library at the university and Joel and I sat out on the lawn for a while, but things just aren't the same. Everyday everything seems to get a little worse. I wish Joel could have been Dad's son, and that I might never have been born.

June 12

Tonight is the dance, but naturally I won't go. Even George, who used to take me out, now looks at me with disdain or passes me by without even seeing me. Apparently the rumors are growing. I just can't even imagine what they are saying or how to stop them.

(?)

I think the old grass gang is trying to drive me completely insane, and they are almost succeeding. Today Mom and I were in the market and we met Marcie and her mom. While they stopped to talk Marcie turned to me and said, with a beautiful smile on her face, 'Tonight we're having a party and this is your last chance.'

I said 'no thank you' as calmly as I could, but I thought I was going to choke. Her mother was standing about two inches away from her! Then she smiled just as sweetly and said, 'You might as well come because we're going to get you anyway.' Can you believe it? A fifteen-year-old girl from an educated, respected family couldn't be threatening another girl in public, not in the nice, precise vegetable department. I thought I was going to lose my mind; that right then and there my mind was going to fall out on the floor and dissolve.

On the way home, Mom commented about my being so quiet. Then she asked me why I didn't get nice Marcie Green to fix me up every now and then. Nice Marcie Green, ha! Maybe I am losing my mind. Maybe these things really aren't happening.

June 16

Gran died in her sleep last night. I tried to tell myself that she's gone to Gramps, but I'm so depressed all I can think about is worms eating her body. Empty eye sockets with whole colonies of writhing maggots. I can no longer eat. The whole house is crazy with everyone worrying about the funeral. Poor Mom, two parents in two months! How can she stand it? I think I'd die if I lost my parents right now. I've been trying to help her and to make things easier, but I'm so exhausted I have to force myself to take every step.

June 17

Joel heard about Gran dying and called to tell me how sorry he was. He really gave me a lot of strength and offered to come over tomorrow after the funeral. I'm so glad he's coming. I'm going to need him.

June 19

I think the one thing that helped me hold on today was knowing that Joel would be waiting. Everytime I wanted to cry I kept thinking about him sitting in our living room and it made things better. I wish Mom had had something to think about because she was really upset. I've never seen her in such bad shape. Dad tried his best, but I don't think he really reached her.

When we got home, Joel and I sat in the back yard and talked for a long time. His father died when he was seven and since then he's thought a lot about death and about life. His feelings and ideas are so mature I can hardly believe he isn't a hundred thousand years old! He's also a very spiritual kind of person, not really religious but spiritual, and he feels very deeply. I think most kids in our generation do. Even on drug trips, many kids think they see God or that they are communing with heavenly things. Anyway when Joel left, he kissed me very tenderly on the lips for the first time. He is so good and fine that I hope someday we can have each other. I really do.

The worst thing about today was seeing soft, frail Gran lowered into that dark, endless hole. It seemed to swallow her up and when they threw dirt on the coffin, I thought I was going to scream. But Joel said not to think about that because that isn't what death really means and I guess he's right. I just can't think about it.

June 20

There are many social things going on now that school is out, and I try not to be hurt because I can't be included. I guess it's sort of indecent to want to go now that Gran has just died. But to tell you the truth, dear friend Diary, I'm tired of being left out and pretending it doesn't hurt. I'm so tired that sometimes I just want to run away again and never come back.

June 22

Last night a bunch of kids were picked up at a party and today they're blaming it on me. Jan rubbed up against me in the drugstore and told me that this time I wasn't going to get away with this finking shit. I tried to tell her that I didn't know anything about it, but as usual she wouldn't listen.

I don't know what I'm going to do if they start on me again. I really don't think I can take it, even with Joel and my family behind me. It's just too much.

June 23

Everything is wrong and I can't go on anymore. I really can't! Today I was just walking down the street by the park when a boy I don't even know grabbed me and threatened me. He kept pulling on my arm and twisting it and calling me every rotten thing in the world. Lots of kids were walking by and I wanted to scream but I couldn't. Who would help me? The straight kids don't even know I'm alive. Then he pushed me around to the back of the clump of bushes and kissed me. It was totally humiliating and disgusting. He pushed his tongue into my mouth and he just kept rolling it around until I was crying and gagging. Then he said that all I needed was a good fuck and that I'd better not tell anyone or he'd come back and really talk things over with me.

I was so frightened I ran to Mr ———'s law office

and asked him to drive me home. He and Mom thought I was sick and she put me to bed. I am sick. Even now I can't stop throwing up and I can't concentrate. What am I going to do? What am I going to do? I can't tell Mom, after Gran and Gramps this would be the last straw. Oh, what am I going to do!

A car just drove by with its lights flashing and the horn blaring and the whole family ran outside to see what was going on, except me. I don't care anymore.

June 24

This morning at breakfast I told the family that I was really being pushed again by the kids. Dad offered to go and talk to some of the parents, but I begged him not to because it would just make things worse. I even told Dad to lock his car because someone threatened to plant marijuana in it. Of course, I had to warn Tim and Alex again, but nothing helps. I feel like we're under siege and no one else seems to be taking it very seriously. Dad really thinks the kids are just putting me on and that they wouldn't do anything to hurt me. I couldn't tell him what happened yesterday, so I guess I'll just have to let him go on thinking that everything is really okay.

Sweet Mom drove me to the university this afternoon to see Joel. She said she had to pick some things up at Dad's office, but I know she was just being thoughtful. She's really very nice.

After I talked with Joel for a while, I don't know why I did it, but I asked him to walk with me and with a completely disintegrated heart, I told him the partial truth. I didn't mean to tell him, but now I guess I'm glad I did. His reaction was just like I always knew it would be. He said that he really cared about me and that he was sure I could handle it because I was basically a good and strong person. Maybe he just said that because he's going home now that the university renovation is over, but he gave me the gold watch his father had given him and I gave him Gran's ring. It was awful. And now I feel like the grayness in all the gray days in the world.

June 25

Today our area was a nut house with everyone running around preparing for tonight's annual 'School Is Out' bash. None of the grass gang paid the least attention to me and I am glad. Maybe they've got another project. It's strange that a big high school like this can be divided into two completely different worlds which seem to know nothing about each other. Or are there many worlds? Is the school actually like a minor galaxy, with a little world for each minority group and one for the poor kids and one for the rich kids, and one for the dopers, or maybe even one for the privileged dopers and one for the dopers who come from not so wealthy backgrounds? All of us being completely unaware of the other worlds until a person tries to step from one sphere to the other. Is that the sin? Or is the real problem in trying to get back to the original globe? Surely all kids who have experimented with drugs don't have this problem, or do they? I guess I shall find out in the future, at least I can try. Chris was lucky, her folks just moved to a town where no one knew her.

P.S. I saw three of the square kids and they asked me if I were going to the bash and everything. Maybe the ice is breaking. I hope, I hope.

June 27

I didn't wake up until 11:30 and I feel so wonderful I could burst. The birds are chirping outside my window. It's summer, dear friend, and I'm alive and well and happy in my own dear bed. Hooray for me! ! ! ! I think I'm going to go to summer school and take some extra courses. Then maybe next summer I can take some summer classes on the university campus. Won't that be fun!

July 1

Imagine the first day of July. I wish Joel were here to see how lovely everything is. He writes very lonely letters already. His mother sounds sweet, but apparently she isn't very intellectual and he longs to have someone to talk to like my mother and father who are very stimulating. He made me promise to enjoy and appreciate them enough for both of us. I stopped taking piano lessons many months ago and I started again today. My teacher gave me an incredibly difficult concerto, but I guess I'll eventually catch on. I want Joel to be proud of my musical abilities as well as other things!

P.S. Tim and I took a long walk yesterday and we saw Jan at the drugstore and Marcie in the park and neither one of them paid any attention to me. Yahoo! I guess now that school is over they've given up on me. They've given up on me and I can finally be really free. Won't that be the most wonderful of glorious feelings in the entire universe? I'm so happy I could die.

July 3

Today is another beautiful, beautiful day except that Dad got the pictures of Gran's grave and the tombstone which was finally placed there. It's a beautiful tombstone, but I keep wondering how decayed her body is by now, and what about Gramps, his must really be a mess! Someday I'm going to get a book on embalming from the library and see just exactly how these things do happen. I wonder if Mom and Dad and Tim think about these things or is it only me? Do I have a morbid mind because of my past experiences? I guess I don't because Joel said he wondered the same thing when his dad died and he was only seven years old.

July 7

Mrs Larsen broke her leg in an automobile accident and I'm going over there every day to clean the house and cook for Mr Larsen and take care of the baby until Mrs Larsen's mother can get there. (Good practice for the future!) Little Lu Ann is a sweet little thing and I'm going to love it. I gotta go now to start my new job. (I hope Mr Larsen doesn't eat at the hospital all the time because I want to practice cooking.)

See ya.

(?)

My dear precious friend,

I am so grateful that they would let Mom bring you to me in your battered, padlocked little case. I was terribly embarrassed when the nurse made me use the combination and dump both of you out and my extra pencils and pens. But I guess they were just being careful and checking to see that you weren't filled with drugs of one sort or another. I don't even feel real. I must be somebody else. I still can't believe that this has actually happened to me. The window is filled with heavy wires, I guess that is better than bars but I still know that I am in some kind of hospital jail.

I have tried to piece the whole thing together but I can't. The nurses and doctors keep telling me I will feel better, but I still can't get straight. I can't close my eyes because the worms are still crawling on me. They are eating me. They are crawling through my nose and gnawing in my mouth and oh God . . . I must get you back in your case because the maggots are crawling off my bleeding writhing hands into your pages. I will lock you in. You will be safe.

(?)

I am feeling better today. They took the bandages off my hands and changed them and it is no wonder they hurt so much. The whole ends of my fingers have been torn off and two nails have been pulled out completely and the others are torn down almost in half. It hurts to write, but I shall lose my mind if I do not. I wish I could write to Joel, but what could I ever tell him and besides no one could ever read this scrawling since both hands are bandaged like boxing gloves. I am still crawling with worms, but I am beginning to be able to live with them, or am I actually dead and they are just experimenting with my soul?

(?)

The worms are eating away my female parts first. They have almost entirely eaten away my vagina and my breasts and now they are working on my mouth and throat. I wish the doctors and nurses would let my soul die, but they are still experimenting with trying to reunite the body and the spirit.

(?)

Today I woke up feeling rational and sound. I guess the bummer is over. The nurse says I have been here ten days, and when I read back what I have written I really must have been out of it.

(?)

Today my hands were placed under a kind of sunlamp to promote the healing. They haven't given me a mirror yet but I can feel that my face is all clawed up too, and my knees and feet and elbows, in fact most of my body is wrenched and battered and bruised. I wonder if my hands will ever look like hands again. The ends of my fingers look like hamburger cooking under the sunlamp, and they've given me a spray to use to ease the pain. They are no longer bandaged, but I almost wish they were because I have to keep looking closely to be sure they aren't getting wormy.

(?)

A fly got into my room today and I couldn't stop screaming. I was so afraid he was going to lay more maggot eggs on my face and hands and body. It took two nurses to kill him. I can't let flies get on me. Maybe I will have to stop sleeping.

(?)

I just got out of bed and walked to the mirror. I have splints on four toes so I guess they are broken too, but anyway I hardly recognized myself. My face is puffed and swollen and black and blue and scratched, and my hair has been pulled out in big patches till I have completely bald areas. Maybe it isn't really me.

(?)

I refractured two toes getting up so now both feet are in casts. Mom and Dad come by to see me every day, but they don't stay long – there isn't much to say, till I get my mind working again.

(?)

I'm really dizzy but the nurse says that is just from my brain concussion. The worms have almost gone away. I guess the spray kills them.

(?)

I found out how I got the acid. Dad says that someone put it on the chocolate covered peanuts and I guess that's right because I remember eating the peanuts after I'd washed the baby. At the time I thought Mr Larsen had left me a surprise. But now that I think about it I don't remember why I thought Mr Larsen had been there and gone without saying anything. That part is a blank. Actually I'm amazed that I remember anything. But I guess no matter what kind of damage I pile on myself, my mind keeps working. The Doctor says that's normal because it really takes a lot to knock your brains loose permanently. I hope that's right because I feel like I've taken a lot already.

Anyway, I remember that the candy reminded me of Gramps because he was always eating chocolate peanut clusters. And I remember starting to get dizzy and sick to my stomach. I guess I tried to call Mom to ask her to come over and get me and the baby when I realized that somebody somehow had tripped me. It's all very unclear because when I try to think back it's like I'm looking through fuzzy, colored lights but I do remember trying to dial home and taking eternities to get each number to the end. I think the line was busy and I don't really remember what happened next except that I was screaming and Gramps was there to help me, but his body was dripping with blazing multicolored worms and maggots which fell on the floor behind him. He tried to pick me up, but only the skeleton remained of his hands and arms. The rest had been picked clean by wriggling, writhing, slithering, busily eating worms which seethed on his every part. They were eating and they wouldn't stop. His two eye sockets were teeming with white soft-bodied, creeping animals which were burrowing in and out of his flesh and which were phosphorescent and swirled into one another. The worms and parasites started creeping and crawling and running toward the baby's room and I tried to stomp on them and beat them to death with my hands but they multiplied faster than I could kill them. And they began crawling on my own hands and arms and face and body. They were in my nose and my mouth and my throat, choking me, strangling me. Tapeworms, larva, grubs, disintegrating my flesh, crawling on me, consuming me.

Gramps was calling me but I could not leave the baby, nor did I want to go with him for he frightened me and nauseated me. He was so badly eaten I could barely recognize him. He kept pointing to a casket next to his and I tried to get away but thousands of other dead things and people were pushing me inside and forcing the lid down on me. I was screaming and screaming and trying to claw my way out of the casket, but they wouldn't let me go.

From the shape I'm in now I guess when I tried to get the worms off me, hunks of flesh and hair came out in my own hands. How I cracked my head I don't know. Maybe I was trying to beat the bummer out of my skull, I really don't remember it seems like such a long long time ago and writing this down has made me incredibly tired. I have never been so tired in my life.

(?)

Mother and Dad believe that somebody tripped me! They do, they do! They believe me! I have a good idea who it was but I guess there will never be any way of finding out. I must just try to rest and get well as they suggested. I will not think about what happened. Thank God I didn't hurt the baby. Thank you God.

(?)

In a few days I am going to be transferred to another hospital. I was hoping I could go home because my hands are healing and most of the bruises have started to fade. The doctor said it will be a year before my hands are completely better with the two nails really grown out but in just a few more weeks they should be fit to look at.

My face is almost back to normal and little fuzzy hair is beginning to grow on my bald patches. Mama brought some scissors and she and the nurse cut my hair really short, short, short. It's almost like a shag cut and isn't quite professional, but Mama says I can go to the beauty shop and have it trimmed in a week or two or whenever I'm released from the other hospital, besides I wouldn't want anyone to see me looking as dingy as I do now.

I still have nightmares about the worms, but I am trying to control myself and I never mention them anymore. What good would it do? I know they aren't real and everybody else knows they aren't real, still at times they seem so very real that I can even feel the warmth and slimy fat softness of their bodies. And every time my nose or one of my many scabs itches, I have to fight myself to keep from screaming for help.

(?)

Mother brought me a packet of letters from Joel. She had written and told him that I was in the hospital very ill, and he has written every day since. He even called one night on the phone and not wanting to get too involved she told him that I had had kind of a nervous breakdown.

Well, that's one way to put it!

July 22

I could tell Mom had been crying when she came to see me today, so I tried to be very strong and put on a really happy face. It's a good thing I did because they are sending me to an insane asylum, a loony bin, a crazy house, freak wharf, where I can wander around with the other idiots and lunatics. I am so scared I cannot even take a full breath. Daddy tried to explain it all very professionally but it was obvious that he had been completely unhinged by the whole thing. But not as much as I am. No one could be.

He said that when my case was taken before the juvenile judge, Jan and Marcie both testified that I had been trying for weeks to sell them LSD and marijuana and that around school I was a known user and pusher.

Circumstances really were quite against me. I have a

drug record and Daddy said that when Mrs Larsen's neighbor heard me screaming, she and the gardener came over to see what was happening and thinking I had gone insane they locked me in a small closet, ran to check the baby who had apparently also been awakened by my screams, and called the police. By the time they got there I had injured myself severely and was trying to scratch the rough plaster off the walls to get out and had beaten my head against the door until I had a brain concussion and a fractured skull.

Now they are going to send me to the Boobie Hatch which is probably where I belong. Daddy says I probably won't be there long and he will immediately start proceedings to have me released and put into the hands of a good psychiatrist.

Dad and Mom keep calling the place where I'm going a youth center, but they aren't fooling anybody. They aren't even fooling themselves. They are sending me to an insane asylum! And I don't understand how can that be. How is it possible? Other people have bad trips and they don't get sent to an insane asylum. They tell me my worms aren't real and yet they're sending me to a place that's worse than all the coffins and the worms put together. I don't understand why this is happening to me. I think I have fallen off the face of the earth and that I will never stop falling. Oh, please, please don't let them take me. Don't let them put me away with insane people. I'm afraid of them. Please let me go home to my own room and go to sleep. Please God.

July 23

My parole officer came and got me and took me to the State Mental Hospital where I was registered and catalogued and questioned and everything but fingerprinted. Then I was taken to the psychiatrist's office and he talked to me for a little while. But I didn't have anything to say because I couldn't even think. All that kept running through my brain was I'm scared, I'm scared, I'm scared.

Then they took me down a smelly, ugly, dingy, paint-peeling old hallway and through a locked door, which was locked again behind me. My heart was pounding so hard that I thought at any second it would explode and spray the whole hall. I could hear it pounding in my ears and I could hardly get one foot in front of the other.

We walked down an endlessly dark hallway and I got a look at some of the people here and now I know I don't belong here. I can't get over what it feels like to be in a world of crazy people, a whole world of them. On the inside and on the outside. I don't belong here, but I'm here. That's crazy isn't it? So you see, dear friend, my only friend, there's nowhere to go because the whole world is crazy.

July 24

The night was interminable. Anything in the world could happen in here and no one would ever know.

July 25

This morning they woke me up at 6:30 for a breakfast I couldn't eat and bleary eyed and still shivering, I was led down the long dark hall to the big metal door with the barred window in the middle. Keys were clanked into the big lock and we were on the other side. Then the keys were clanked again. The day attendants talked a lot but I really couldn't hear them. My ears are clogged up, probably from fear. Then they took me to the Youth Center which was just two buildings away, passed two slobbering men with another attendant who were raking up leaves.

At the Youth Center there were fifty, sixty, maybe even seventy kids, milling around preparing to go to their classes or whatever they were going to do. All of them seemed pretty normal except one big girl who looked to be about my age but who was eight or ten inches taller and at least fifty pounds heavier. She was stretched out stupidly under the pinball machine in the dayroom, and there was also a teenage boy who kept bouncing his head and muttering idiotically.

A bell rang and all of the kids went off except the two dummies. I was left in the dayroom with them. Finally a large lady (the school nurse) came in and said that if I wanted the privilege of going to school I would have to go see Doctor Miller and sign a commitment that I was ready to live according to all the Center rules and regulations.

I said I was ready but Doctor Miller was not in so I spent the rest of the morning in the day room watching the two dum-dums, one sleeping and one bouncing. I wondered what insane impression I made upon them, with my healing face and my lawn mower type haircut.

All through the endless morning bells rang and people came and went. There was a stack of magazines on a little round table in the hall but I couldn't read them. My mind was racing a thousand miles a minute and going nowhere.

At 11:30 Marj, the nurse, showed me the dining room. Kids were milling around in all directions, and certainly none of them looked crazy enough to be locked up but obviously they all were. The meal consisted of macaroni and cheese with a little bologna cut up in it and canned string beans, and some kind of soggy looking pudding. Trying to eat was a big waste of time. I couldn't get anything down past the lump in my throat.

A lot of the kids were laughing and teasing each other and it was pretty obvious that they even call their teachers and therapists and social workers by their first names. I guess everyone but the doctors. None of them seem as frightened as am I. Were they frightened when they first came here? Are they still frightened but putting up a good front? I don't understand how can they exist here. Truthfully, the Youth Center isn't as bad as the ward. It seems almost like a small school, but the hospital itself is unbearable. The smelly halls, the bleak people, the locked barred doors. It's a dreadful nightmare, it's a bad trip, it's a bummer, it's everything terrible that I can imagine.

Dr Miller finally came back in the afternoon and I got to talk to him. He told me that the hospital couldn't help me, and the staff couldn't help me and the teachers couldn't help me, and the program which had proved very successful couldn't help me, unless I wanted help! He also told me that before I could overcome my problem I had to admit I had a problem, but how can I do that when I really haven't? I know now that I could resist drugs if I were drowning in them. But how will I ever convince anyone other than Mom and Dad and

Tim, and Joel, I hope, that I didn't really take anything knowingly this last time? It sounds incredible that the first time I took drugs and the last time which landed me in an insane asylum were both given to me without my knowledge. Oh nobody would believe anyone could be that dumb. I can hardly believe it myself even when I know it's true.

Anyway how can I admit anything when I am so scared I can't even talk? I just sat nodding my head in Dr Miller's office so I wouldn't have to open my mouth. Nothing would have come out anyway.

At 2:30 the kids were out of school, and some of them went to play ball and part of them stayed here for group therapy.

Some of what the first doctor and the parole officer told me is coming back. The kids are in two groups. Group One kids are trying to obey all the rules and get released. They get all the privileges offered. Group Two is kind of grounded. They aren't obeying the rules, and are losing their tempers or cursing or stealing or having sex or something and so they are restricted in everything. I hope there's no pot here. I know I could resist it, but I don't think I could stand any more problems without really going crazy. I guess the doctors know what they're doing but I'm so lonely and so lost and so frightened. I think I really am losing my mind.

At 4:30 it was time for us to come back to our wards and be locked in again like animals in the zoo. There are six other girls besides myself and five boys who are in my ward, and thank God for that for I couldn't have gone back by myself. However I noticed that they all cringed a little (as I do) when the doors clanked shut behind us.

While we were walking through an older woman said it had been peaceful and quiet till now and the littlest girl turned and said, 'Fuck you.' I was so surprised I looked for the ceiling to fall down on her head, but no one seems to pay any attention but me.

July 26

The little girl I told you about yesterday is in the room next to mine. She's thirteen and she seems constantly on the verge of tears. When I asked her how long she'd been here, she said, 'Forever, simply forever.'

At dinner time she walked with me to the place where we eat and we sat together, not eating, at one of the long tables. The rest of the evening we were left to wander around the ward with nowhere to go and nothing to do. I desperately want to tell Mom and Dad what it's like here but I won't. It would only make them worry more.

One older woman in the ward is a lecherous alcoholic and she frightens me but I'm worried even more for Babbie. What's to keep this dirty creature from making passes at us? She made some gestures when we passed her tonight and I asked Babbie if we couldn't do something about her. But Babbie just shrugged and said we could report her to the attendant but that it was better just to ignore her.

Then something really weird and terrifying happened. We were sitting in one of the 'recreation' rooms watching the others watch us. It was like monkeys watching monkeys and when I asked Babbie if she wouldn't rather talk in my room, she said we weren't allowed to have sex in our rooms but we could manage it in the storeroom tomorrow. I didn't know what to say! She thought I was trying to seduce her and I was so stunned I couldn't say anything. Later I tried to explain but she just started talking about herself as if I wasn't even there.

She said she's thirteen and that she had been on drugs for two years. Her parents were divorced when she was ten and she was sent to live with her father who's a contractor and who's remarried. I guess things were all right for a while but she was jealous of her new mother's children and felt like an outsider, a stranger. Then she began spending more and more time away from home, telling her stepmother that she was having trouble with school and had to go to the library, etc. The usual excuses, when actually she was going to school about only half the time. But she was still bringing home good grades so her parents didn't seem too interested. Finally the school called because she was out so much. But she told her father that the school was so big and crowded, they didn't know who was there and who wasn't. I don't know why her father believed that one, but I guess he did. It was probably too much trouble not to.

Anyway what really was going on was that Babbie had been introduced to drugs by some thirty-two-year old man she met in a matinee movie. She didn't tell me the details but I guess he introduced her to drugs and to the life in general. A few months later he floated away and she found that it was very easy to meet other men. In fact at twelve she was already a BP.* She told me all of this so quietly I felt like ripping my heart out. But even if I'd cried (which I didn't), I don't think she would have noticed, she was so out of it.

After she had been on drugs for a about a year, her bright-eyed parents began to become suspicious. But even then they didn't deal with her head on. They just started asking a lot of questions and bugging her, so she robbed the next man she met at the movies and took a

_____

* baby prostitute

bus to L.A. A friend had told her that it was never any trouble for BPs to get by and, according to Babbie, the friend was right. On her second day in L.A., she was wandering around and she met a 'friend,' a beautifully dressed woman who took her to a big apartment on _____ Boulevard. When she got there, there were some girls her age in the living room and pills all over the place in candy dishes. Within a half an hour, she was completely stoned.

Later, when she came back down, the woman said she could live there and go to school. She said she only had to work for her two hours a day – mostly in the afternoons. So the next day she registered in school as the woman's niece and began living as a high class BP. The woman had four nieces staying with her while Babbie lived there. The chauffeur took them to school and picked them up and they never saw any of the money they made. Babbie said they just sat in the apartment like monkeys most of the time, never really talking and never going anywhere.

It sounded so unbelievable that I tried to ask her questions, but she kept right on talking and she was so sad and distant that I think she was really telling the truth. Besides after what I've been through, I think I'd believe anything. Isn't that sad, to be in a spot where everything is so unbelievable you'd believe anything? I think it's sad, dear friend, I really and truly and desperately do.

Anyway, after a few weeks Babbie ran away and hitch-hiked to San Francisco. But in San Francisco, four guys beat her up and raped her. When she tried to panhandle some money to call home, no one would give her any. She said she would have crawled home and let them chain her in a closet but when I asked her why she hadn't gone to the police or to a hospital, she just started yelling and spitting on the floor.

Later I guess she finally reached her parents, but by the time they got to San Francisco she had wandered off with some guy who had set up his own lab to make LSD. They both got mixed up in some communal shit and eventually she landed here, just like me.

Oh, Diary, I'm so grateful I have you because there is nothing, absolutely nothing to do in this animal cage and everyone is so crazy that I know I couldn't exist without you.

There is a woman somewhere down the hall who moans and groans and makes unearthly noises. Even putting my sick, broken hands over my ears and the pillow over my head doesn't keep out the horrible gurgling sounds. Will I ever again in my whole life be able to sleep without having to keep my tongue between my teeth to stop the chattering and without having terror flood in upon my mind when I think of this place? It can't be real! I'm still on my bad trip. I must be. I think they are going to bring busloads of school children by tomorrow to feed us peanuts through the bars.

July 27

Dear Diary,

I truly must have lost my mind or at least control of it, for I have just tried to pray. I wanted to ask God to help me but I could utter only words, dark, useless words which fell on the floor beside me and rolled off into the corners and underneath the bed. I tried, I really tried to remember what I should say after, 'Now I lay me down to sleep . . .' but they are only words, useless, artificial, heavy words which have no meaning and no powers. They are like the ravings of the idiotic spewing woman who is now part of my inmate family. Verbal rantings, useless, groping, unimportant, with no power and no glory. Sometimes I think death is the only way out of this room.

July 29

I was allowed the privilege of going to school today, and here school is a privilege. Nothing could be darker or bleaker or barer than just sitting with nothing to do and millions of endless hours in which to do it.

I must have cried in my sleep because this morning my pillow was soggy and wet, and I have been completely exhausted. The junior high kids have two teachers and we have two. They both seem kind and most of the kids seem pretty controlled. I guess that's because they're afraid of being sent again to no-mansland, a world of wandering and being alone.

I guess people can adjust to anything, even to being locked up in an institution. Tonight when they locked the huge heavy door I didn't even feel too terribly depressed or maybe I am just cried out.

Babbie and I sat and talked for a while and I put up her hair, but all the joy and spontaneity has gone out of life. I am beginning to drag and merely exist as she does.

The other girls on the ward talk and joke and watch TV and sneak into the bathrooms to smoke, but Babbie and I are just trying to keep ourselves together.

Everybody smokes here and the halls are filled with fumes and gray circling smoke, there isn't even anywhere for it to go. It seems as trapped and confused as the patients.

The attendants all wear heavy clanking keys pinned to their aprons. The constant sound of them jangling together is a continual depressing reminder.

July 30

Tonight Babbie went down to the dayroom to watch TV and I am jealous. Will I wind up a hard butch angry at some child who has given her affection to an old woman with a package of cigarettes to share with her?

This can't be! It can't be happening to me!

July 31

After school today we had group therapy in the Youth Center dayroom. It was very interesting listening to the kids. I was dying to ask how all the kids had felt when they first came here, but I didn't dare open my mouth. Rosie was upset because she felt the kids were ignoring her and they all told her why she wasn't easy to be with: because she tried to monopolize people and was always clinging to them and hanging on to them. At first she was angry and swore, but I think before it was over she understood herself a little better, at least she should have.

Then they discussed how others were 'feeding their own problems' which was interesting. Perhaps the time I am spending here will actually make me a more capable person.

After therapy, Carter, who is the present president of

the group (they vote a new one each six weeks), sat and talked with me. He told me to feel free to bring my thoughts and angers and fears out in the open to be examined. He told me that clumped inside they all seemed magnified and distorted out of true proportion. And he also said that when he first came here he had been scared so badly that for three days he literally lost his voice. He physically couldn't talk! He was sent here basically because no one could deal with him. He had been in juvenile halls and reform schools and foster homes so many times he couldn't count them, but the thought of being in a mental hospital really blew his mind.

He told me we could get out of Group Two once we made some progress and proved we were under control. He'd been in Group One a couple of times, but always got sent back because of his temper. He also said that in two weeks the Group One kids were going on a bus trip to a cave in the mountains and on a tour through the cave. Oh, I want to go on that trip. I've got to get out of here! I've simply got to.

August 1

Today Mom and Dad came to visit me. They still believe me and Dad has been to see Jan and feels that he will soon be able to get her at least to take back the statement that I was trying to sell her drugs.

I am so grateful for group therapy. Maybe now I'll get something out of this place instead of being broken by it.

August 2

I had a session with Doctor Miller and I think he believes me too! He seems delighted that I want to go into social work and feels there is a great need for people who understand what's going on out there. He suggested that I ask some of the kids here about their backgrounds which maybe would give me more insight into people but he warned me not to be shocked at some of the things I should find out. I guess he thinks there are still things in this world that might amaze me. It's a good thing he doesn't know all of my background, at least I think he doesn't? ? ?

At first I felt I would be too shy to ask kids outright to tell me about themselves. But he said if I told the kids why I wanted to know he was sure they would want to help me. I'm still not sure I want to go prying into other people's lives. I'm not at all sure I'd want to tell them about mine. I guess I would though – except maybe the very worst parts.

I watched TV for a little while tonight, but there are

only six kids on this ward and thirty older ladies, and since we have to vote on which programs we can see, naturally they win.

I think I'd rather read or write anyway. I'm trying to get Babbie to read and maybe she will get a book from the Youth Center library tomorrow if I push her. It certainly will help take her mind off things, if she can concentrate. Her social worker is trying to get her into a foster home, but with her background it seems to be difficult, and apparently her parents don't want her anymore. Isn't that sad!

August 3

It's been a beautiful, hot lazy day. We were lying out on the lawn when I got the courage to ask Tom _____, who is in the men's section of my ward, why he was in.

Tom is a handsome, likeable, extremely articulate young guy. He's fifteen and he's the kind of person people automatically feel comfortable around. He said he came from a solid, comfortable, unbroken home and in his last year of junior high school he was voted best liked kid in his school. I guess I would be voted biggest idiot if they did that kind of thing in our school.

Anyway last spring, he and three of his buddies heard about sniffing glue and thought it sounded exciting so they bought a couple of tubes and tried it.

He said they made a lot of noise yelling and rolling around on the floor, and the kid's dad yelled down and told them to cool it. He didn't even suspect why they were cutting up. He just thought they were scuffling around like they always did.

A week later the same three tried his Dad's Scotch, but they didn't like it as much and found it was harder to get than pot and pills. He said what I'd heard before, that parents never miss their diet pills, their tranquilizers, their cold remedies, their pep pills, their sleeping pills, or any of the other things that will supply kids with a 'jolt' when they can't get their hands on anything else. So he started easy, but in six months he said he needed so much money that he had to get a job. So he applied at the most logical place – a drugstore. And it took the manager a fairly long time to figure out what was happening to his pill supply. When he did, he 'laid Tommy off' to save his family embarrassment. Nothing was ever said and nobody but Tommy and the manager knew what was going on. However, even getting fired was okay with Tommy because by this time he was into hard drugs and really didn't care very much what happened. A friend had introduced him to Smack and he started pushing at the Junior High to keep himself going. Then he ended up here, and in my green opinion he's still freaked out, for even now he almost has a contact high just talking about drugs. I noticed that Julie, who was sitting fairly close to us, had almost the same reaction. It's sort of like watching someone yawn. You're drawn into it and you start yawning yourself. I'm so grateful I felt nothing, but I almost wish I hadn't asked because it was really depressing to see that he and Julie can't wait to get out of here and get back on their thing.

Oh, I hate it here! The dirty bathroom urine smells. The small barred cages where people are locked up if they get out of line. One old lady who is a firebug is in one of the cages almost all the time, and I can't stand it. The people are the very worst of all.

August 4

Today we went swimming. On the way back on the bus I sat with Margie Ann who said she doesn't ever want to get out. She said as soon as she gets out the kids will be right there hassling her head and trying to get her to take off again and right now she knows she couldn't say no. Then she looked at me and said, 'Why don't we take off, just the two of us. I know where we can get a mixed bag in a minute.'

August 5

Mom and Dad came to visit again today and they brought me a ten page letter from Joel. Mom wanted me to read it right away but I wanted to wait until I was alone. It's very special to me and I really don't want to share it with anybody but you. Besides I think I'm a little scared because Dad told Joel the truth about me, at least as much as he knows. So I think I'll wait until later to open it.

Dad also said that he finally got Jan to sign an affidavit saying that I wasn't pushing at the school. Now both she and Dad are trying to get Marcie to retract her statement. Dad says if that happens he's sure he can get me out of here in no time.

I'm afraid to hope but I can't help it, and the idea of hoping in this most hopeless of all places makes me want to cry.

Later

Joel's letter was great. I was really afraid to read it but now I'm happy that I did. He is the most warm, compassionate, forgiving, loving, most understanding person in the world, and I can't wait for fall when we can be together again. I know I won't have any more drug problems, but I'm such a boob, such an immature, childish, impractical, improbable wishy-washy that I'm really going to have to work to make Joel proud of me. Oh, I wish he were here right now and I wish I were strong like the rest of my family. I wish, I wish, I wish.

August 8

Oh, glorious, marvelous, wonderful, incredible, fantastic day! Day with birds and singing and sunshine and flowers! I can't tell you how happy I am. I'm getting out of here! I'm going HOME! All the papers will be signed today and Dad and Mom will come and get me tomorrow. Oh, lifetime away tomorrow. I feel like screaming with joy but that would probably make them come and lock me up again. Actually I'm not being fair to this place. As awful as it is, it's better than detention school. Kay said that if she had been sent to DT* she would have learned every rotten trick in the book. Here, she

---

* detention school

sticks to the ones she already knows. I guess that's pretty true with all of us.

I can't believe I'm really going home. Somebody up there must be pulling for me. Probably dear old Gramps.

Later

I couldn't sleep, so I woke up and began thinking about Babbie. I really feel guilty that I'm going and she's staying. Maybe when I'm really strong and the nightmare of my life fades a little, we can come back and get her. But I guess that's just being childish. Life doesn't really happen that way, which is too bad. But I can't think about it anymore.

August 9

At last, finally and forever, I'm home. Tim and Alex were so glad to see me that I really felt rotten for having messed up so badly all these months. Then when Happiness came up and licked my face and hands, I thought Mother was going to cry and I was just glad that Gran and Gramps aren't alive to see what's happened.

I guess Dad knew how I felt, because he was so loving and dear. Dear, dear Dad, he always knows. And after we had all talked for a while, he suggested that I go up and get some sleep which was really great because I wanted to be completely alone in my own room with my own lovely curtains and my own wallpaper and my own bed and feel my own house all around me with my beautiful, loving family downstairs. I'm so very, very grateful that they don't hate me, because in a lot of ways I hate myself.

August 10

Dear Diary,

It's 2 A.M. and I've just had the sweetest feeling I've ever had in my life. I tried to pray again. Actually I was just trying to thank God for getting me out of there and bringing me home but then I started to think about Jan and Marcie and for the first time I really wanted God to help them too. I really wanted them to get completely well and not to have to end up in a mental hospital. Oh, please God, I hope they do get well. Please help them and help me too.

August 12

Dad has a chance to go back East for two weeks to finish a lecture course, isn't that marvelous? Of course it isn't marvelous for Dr _____ who has had a heart attack, and I really hope he gets better; but anyway, Daddy is going to fill in for him at the last minute, and we're all going to stay in their gorgeous house and everything, isn't that great?

August 14

They only had one double room left in the motel so Alex and I have one bed and Mom and Daddy have the other and Tim has to sleep on the floor because they don't even have any more cots left. He doesn't mind, though – he says it's like camping out. We're drawing lots to see who gets to use the bathroom first. I was last, but that's okay because I wanted to write in you.

Everything would be absolutely perfect if only Joel were here. He is the only good thing missing in our lives, but I guess that would be a little messy, all sharing the same room and bath and us not even married. It might be even more embarrassing if we were – but I won't even let myself think about that. There will absolutely be no more sex in my life until after I have taken a man for better or for worse until death do us part, and then I even think we'll still be together. I just simply can't imagine a just God making people who love each other be single after they get to Heaven. Gran and Gramps and Mother and Dad could never possibly be happy unless they were together. I'm sure Gran died because she just couldn't bear being separated. There wasn't a single thing wrong with her except that she didn't want to go on without Gramps.

I wonder if Mom ever even kissed another man besides Dad. Oh, I'm sure she did, because Dad sometimes teases her about Humphrey, but I know she wasn't having sex with Humphrey. I don't think many girls did things like that when Mom and Gran were young. I wish things were still like that. I think it would be much easier to be a virgin, marry someone and then find out what life is all about. I wonder how it will be for me? It might be great because I'm practically a virgin in the sense that I've never had sex except when I've been stoned and I'm sure without drugs I'll be scared out of my mind. I just hope I can forget everything that's happened when I finally get married to someone I love. That's a nice secure thought, isn't it? Going to bed with someone you love.

It's my turn in the bathroom so I gotta go.

See ya.

August 17

Well, we're settled. Daddy starts teaching today, and this afternoon we're going to take a look at the town. It was dark when we drove in, but this neighborhood is incredible, everything is all lush and green and fragrant. I'm so happy we're here. We're all exhausted though because yesterday and the night before Mom and Dad took turns driving straight through. Two days and one night of driving put us all a little on edge, and while it was fun and interesting to see parts of the country we're still glad to be settled. Daddy says we'll take longer to go home and maybe even go by way of Chicago, and stop to see Joel. Wouldn't that be wonderful! ! ! I'm afraid to even uncross my fingers to eat or write.

August 20

Imagine me at a university tea! And even more startling, imagine me liking it even though it was a little stuffy. I must be growing up.

See ya.

August 22

Well, there will be no more exploring for wonder woman! Apparently I walked into a giant batch of poison ivy yesterday and really did it to myself. There isn't too much of it around here, but wouldn't you know who'd find it!

I'm swollen and red and itching all over, and my eyes are puffed up and almost closed and I really look great. The doctor came and gave me a shot, but he doesn't sound too encouraging. Yuck!

August 24

I didn't know P.I. was so contagious, but now Alex has gotten it off my clothes or something. She isn't as bad as I am, but she's still itchy and uncomfortable. Some people from the university came to find out where I'd run across the clump so they could go out and kill it, but I don't even know what it looks like.

August 27

Hooray! We're going to New York for the weekend. Mom and Tim and Alex and I are taking the train tomorrow and we won't be back until Monday. Isn't that great? All the stores and everything – I can't wait. My P.I. is down to pink spots, and I'm sure my makeup can cover that. I hope, I hope. We're taking the 7:15 train tomorrow, and Dad says I can buy a lot of new things for school. Hooray! Hooray!

August 29

It's so hot and stuffy in Manhattan I can't believe it. We're fine as long as we stay in the big stores, but when we're out on the street it's like walking in a furnace. The heat comes up from the sidewalk in great clouds and I don't know how the people who live there stand it. Joel says it's as bad in Chicago, but I find that hard to believe. Anyway, we spent most of the morning shopping at Bloomingdale's and then went to a movie at Radio City in the afternoon just to get out of the heat.

Taking the subway was the biggest mistake we ever made. It was so jammed with humanity that we were tangled like sauerkraut in a jar and smelled just as bad. One fat old woman was hanging on a strap beside me and her sleeveless dress exposed the most incredible bird's nest under her arm. It was the smelliest sight I witnessed in my life. I hope Tim didn't see it or he'll probably be turned off women forever.

Tomorrow we're going to the Museum of Modern Art and a couple of other places. I don't think we'll stay late on Sunday because Mother is as uncomfortable as we are.

September 2

We are not going through Chicago after all. They are making staff changes at the university and Dad has got to get back. He offered to go out of his way and make a quick stop in Chicago because he didn't want to let me down, but I can't be that immature – besides, I'll see Joel in just a few weeks, and we're not engaged or anything. I wish we were!

September 4

Driving all day and almost all night is really a drag. Dad looks absolutely bug-eyed, and Alex is squirming all over the place. I really wish I could help with the driving, but Dad says absolutely no driving without a license, which I'm going to get as soon as I can.

One more billboard and I'm going to lose my mind!

September 6

Home at last. Poor Dad has to go over to the university and I know he is absolutely beat. If I'm as tired as I am at my age I don't know how he even manages to get one foot in front of the other. Mother is dashing around the house chipper as a little bird, but I guess that is because she's HOME, HOME, HOME. Oh what a beautiful, wonderful, divinely lovely word.

I'm even beginning to feel pretty good myself. Just a few hours ago none of us thought we could possible live for even a few more minutes, now we're all getting our second wind. Alex has dashed off to Tricia's to pick up Honey and her kittens and Happiness, and Tim is puttering around in his 'stink room' as Alex calls it, and I'm doing what I love most, just enjoying myself in my own lovely room with my books and all my personal possessions. I just can't decide what to do first, go play my lovely piano or stay here and curl up with a lovely book or take a lovely nap.

I think the nap is going to win.

September 7

I met Fawn _____ at the store today and she invited me to come over tonight and go swimming in their pool. Isn't that lovely? Maybe I can get back in with the straight kids this year and then the dopey dopers wouldn't dare bother me. Wouldn't that be perfect? Anyway, Fawn and her sisters all do water ballet and I'm not a very good swimmer but she promised to teach me. I hope I don't drown or fall on my head in the shallow end of the pool.

September 10

I don't know why I have to be so insecure and frightened. I haven't even known Fawn very long and yet I'm almost jealous of all her other friends. I think they're prettier and smarter and that no one really wants me around which is pretty stupid since they keep inviting me over there all the time. I guess I'm just a jerk. I just hope none of them has heard all the rotten stories that went around about me. I really don't know who Jan and Marcie and all those dopey dopers spoke to, but I hope it wasn't the whole school. Oh, I hope I'm not going to be hurt again. I wonder if all girls are as timid as I am? If I think a boy might ask me out I'm scared to death he won't and if he actually does then I'm afraid to go.

Like last night we were all swimming and a carload of boys drove up and Fawn's father, who's really nice, asked them to come in and have some punch. So we all clowned around for a while and then turned the hose on the patio and danced on the wet cement. It was fun and I guess I looked pretty cute because Frank _____ asked me out. Actually he wanted to take me home, but I wanted to stay and help Fawn clean up. But I guess the truth is I just don't feel myself around boys anymore. Mother says it's just because I feel frightened and unsure again and I hope she's right. I do hope she's right!

September 11

Fawn called up the first thing this morning. She wants to have a party next Friday and invite boys. I'm going over this afternoon to help her plan it but I really would rather not get involved. Wally asked her out last night too, and she's going to the movies with him tonight. I sort of wish she wouldn't. I don't know why I worry about her, she's a few months older than I am, but I just think boys are the root of most problems. At least, they've been at the root of most of mine, which is probably a big lie. Anyway, this morning I was reading an article on identity and responsibility, and it said that kids who aren't allowed to make any decisions for themselves never grow up, and kids who have to make all the decisions before they're ready never grow either. I don't think I fall into either category but it's an interesting idea.

See ya.

September 16

Guess what? Mrs ———— , my old piano teacher, called and she wants me to be soloist at her outstanding student recital. She even wants to get the small auditorium at the University and do all the publicity and everything with *my* picture on the program cover. Of course, she knows about my hands so it wouldn't be until later on in the fall, but isn't that exciting! I didn't know I was that good! I really and truly and honestly didn't!

She wants to meet with my parents some night soon and discuss the whole idea, but frankly I'm still flying. I can't believe it's true. I mean I practice every day and sometimes I sit down and play just for fun if there isn't anything else to do, but that's mostly because I don't like the tube, especially the stuff Tim and Alex want to watch, and I can't read forever. I really didn't realize I was that good. I wonder if the kids will think it's a stupid thing to do. I certainly don't want to screw things up with them, particularly now when we're starting to develop such a great relationship. I think I'll just wait and talk the whole thing over with Fawn, but I'll wait until after her party. I know that's the first thing on her mind right now.

P.S. I got the loveliest of all letters from Joel and he can't wait to see me. I didn't tell him that that's the way I feel too but I'm sure he knows.

September 17

Wouldn't you know, I got my period! Now I'll be self-conscious about that too! I wonder if Mother would be upset if I bought Tampax instead of just plain Kotex? She probably would be, so I guess I'd better not take the chance – but it really does mess things up for tomorrow night. Oh, I guess it really doesn't matter. I can always wear my new plaid pants and my new top, but it really is a drag.

Oh, well, there's nothing I can do about it, so I might as well be cheerful. Right?

Nite.

September 18

I looked at the sky this morning and realized that summer is almost gone which really made me sad because it doesn't seem as though it's been here at all. Oh, I don't want it to be over. I don't want to get old. I have this very silly fear, dear friend, that one day I'll be old, without ever having really been young. I wonder if it could happen that quickly or if I've ruined my life already. Do you think life can get by you without your even seeing it? Cripes, it gives me chills just thinking about it.

(?)

Boy, am I a dummy! Tomorrow is Dad's birthday and I had completely forgotten it. Tim and Mom planned an outing, just for the family, but I was so wrapped up with Fawn and the rest of the kids that they didn't want to bother me with the details, which shows you who the creep is around this house. Oh well, there's no point in kicking myself about it. I'll just have to think up something super special for Dad and surprise everyone.

See ya.

September 19

Mom was right. My premonitions about Fawn's party were completely ridiculous. It was great, great, great. Fawn's parents are really nice and all the kids there are the really great ones. Jess _____ is going to be next year's student council president and Tess is the girl's president and Judy and just everyone. I remember a year ago thinking they were a bunch of dull squares but now I just hope they'll give me another chance and not bounce me on my head.

I suspect if I were really mature I would accept the fact that sooner or later someone is going to start talking about my being picked up even though it was simply ages ago, and then every nice kid's parents will tell them that they shouldn't spend any time with me because I will ruin their reputation. And every nice kid will wonder what I'm really like inside, and if they hear that I was in a mental hospital, I can just imagine what will go around in their heads and out their mouths! You'd think with over 900 kids in this school I could swing from one side to the other, and I can if they'll let me! Oh, I can! Please, please let me!

Maybe I should really be honest about it and tell Fawn and her parents. Do you think they would understand, or would it just embarrass us all? I know sooner or later I've just got to tell Fawn about the hospital. She's already asked me about my hands and I just don't feel decent about lying to her anymore. I wish I knew what to do. If I had someone who knew how to handle these things I wouldn't have to sit here in my bed and worry you and myself. They could just say right out, 'You should do this or that.' I'm sure Mother and Dad are even more uncertain about these things than I am. They tried to keep it as quiet as possible, and I'm not sure any of their close friends even know what happened. Why is life so difficult? Why can't we just be ourselves and have everyone accept us the way we are? Why can't I just be *me* as I am now and not have to concentrate and fume and get upset about my past and my future. I hate never knowing whether tomorrow I'm going to have Jan and Lane and Marcie and all the rest on my back, sometimes I wish I had never been born.

I wonder what nice Frank would think if he knew about the real inside me? He'd probably run like a scared rabbit or immediately think he could get anything he wanted, and he'd want only one thing!

I do wish I could sleep. Isn't it weird how sometimes time goes so fast you can't even keep up with it, like it's been going the last two or three weeks. Hours and minutes and days and weeks and months merge into one another in a flashing blur. Dad's birthday is today and tomorrow is mine. A hundred years ago, I'd probably have been married by now and out on a farm somewhere begetting children. I guess I'm lucky things don't happen quite that quickly these days. But in any case, I've got to start behaving and thinking more like an adult.

Later

Oh, this afternoon I ran out and got Dad a sleeveless sweater. I'm sure he'll like it because he saw something very similar in Mr Taylor's window and said that it would be just perfect for the office when he doesn't want to wear a coat. Now I just have to finish the poem and at least I'll have done something right. I wonder if life is as explosive and confusing to other people. I hope not, because I really wouldn't wish this mess on anyone else.

I wonder if they'll include my birthday party with Dad's tonight or if they'll have a separate one later? Two birthday cakes in one week might make everyone sick.

Gee, another birthday! I'll be almost an old woman, at least more than half way through my teens. It seems only yesterday I was a child.

September 20

I barely had my eyes open when Frank called to ask me out for tonight but I told him I would be busy with my family the whole weekend. He seemed disappointed, but I think he believed me. Anyway I can smell a whole vat of bacon cooking downstairs and I'm so hungry I could eat my quilt.

See ya.

P.S. Dad's birthday was super! Everyone was so close and warm and we had such a wonderful time but I'll tell you more about it later.

P.P.S. He loved the sweater and my poem. I think he liked the poem especially because I wrote it for him personally. He even blew his nose when he read it.

Later
Everybody's downstairs plotting and the whole house is filled with mouth-watering fragrances fit for kings and exotic princesses. I wonder what they're doing. Mother and Tim and Alex wouldn't even let me come in the living room. They told me to go right upstairs and take a bath and set my hair and not to come down until I was the most beautiful creature in the world. I don't know how they expect me to manage that but it will be fun trying.

Later
You will never, ever guess what happened! Joel was here! I knew he was registering late because of his job but . . . Well, I still can't believe it. The meanie. He's been here four whole days and he was actually down in the living room when I came home this afternoon wearing my old cut offs and Daddy's oldest sweat shirt covered with white paint. He said when I dragged up the path, he was

215

almost ready to turn around and go back to Chicago; thank heavens I changed into my white dress and new sandals. He couldn't believe I was the same person. Tim and Dad laughed and said they'd had to tie him to a chair to make him stay after he saw me the first time.

It was a fun, fun night, and I'm sure they were kidding, I hope! Anyway, when Joel saw me he kissed me right on the lips in front of my whole family and hugged me till I thought my insides and backbone were crunching like potato chips. It was lovely even though it was a little embarrassing.

They had been planning this all summer and I thought my birthday was just going to be sort of leftovers from Daddy's. Instead of that it was the nicest one I've ever had. Joel gave me a white enameled friendship ring with little flowers all over it and I shall wear it until I die. I have it on right now and it's truly lovely. Mother and Dad gave me the new leather jacket I've been wanting and Tim gave me a scarf and Alex made me some peanut brittle, which Daddy and Joel and Tim ate to get even with me for eating most of Dad's on his birthday. Funny little Alex, she can make better peanut brittle than either Mom or me, and she knows it and won't tell us what her secret is, maybe it's just because she's so sweet and part of her rubs off on the peanuts.

I only got to see Joel alone for about ten minutes when we sat on the porch steps before Dad drove him back to wherever he's staying. I even forgot to ask we had so much to talk about but I'm sure he likes me in a quiet, soft, gentle, permanent, lasting way. We held hands most of the evening, but that didn't mean too much because Alex was hanging on to the other one and Tim kept trying to drag him off to show him all the things he'd collected over the summer.

Well, if I'm going to get up and practice at six and face tomorrow I'd better get some sleep. Besides I want to dream about lovely today and how much more lovely every day after today is going to be.

September 21

I woke up even before the alarm went off. It's only five minutes after five and I doubt that anyone else on this block is up, but I am so wide awake I can barely stand it. Frankly, I think I'm scared witless inside about going back to school but in my head I know it's going to be all right because I have Joel and my new super straight friends and they'll help me. Besides I'm much stronger than I used to be. I know I am.

I used to think I would get another diary after you are filled, or even that I would keep a diary or journal through my whole life. But now I don't really think I will. Diaries are great when you're young. In fact, you saved my sanity a hundred, thousand, million times. But I think when a person gets older she should be able to discuss her problems and thoughts with other people, instead of just with another part of herself as you have been to me. Don't you agree? I hope so, for you are my dearest friend and I shall thank you always for sharing my tears and heartaches and my struggles and strifes, and my joys and happinesses. It's all been good in its own special way, I guess.

See ya.

Epilogue

The subject of this book died three weeks after her decision not to keep another diary.

Her parents came home from a movie and found her dead. They called the police and the hospital but there was nothing anyone could do.

Was it an accidental overdose? A premeditated overdose? No one knows, and in some ways that question isn't important. What must be of concern is that she died, and that she was only one of approximately 50,000 drug deaths in the United States that year.

WHAT DEFEATED ALICE?
A Psychologist's Comment

This is a rare and unusual document, based on a diary kept by an adolescent who has sufficient power over language to convey the realities of adolescent experience. This diary, like the classic of its kind, the diary of Anne Frank, has much to teach us about the struggles adolescents go through, the frequent turmoil of their inner worlds – often masked from observers – and their quandary about how to relate to the self-absorbed, but nearly always well-meaning, adults around them. It has particular point at present because it shows us how one girl got drawn inadvertently into the drug scene, and how she struggled to free herself. We must ask why it all turned out so tragically. Many young people *do* have a brush with drugs and make good their escape. Why not Alice?

There are, I think, some important lessons to be learnt. The first is that *any* adolescent *may* get caught up with the drug set. If young people are out and about at all – and we cannot lock up our children – then the *possibility* of becoming involved is likely to occur. Drug-users are by no means all sleazy ne'er-do-wells. The drug scene includes pleasant and intelligent young people.

We notice that Alice's parents warmly approved of some of her drug-taking friends, no doubt hoping that they would help to 'bring her out'.

Living as we do in a drug-consuming age – mountains of sleeping pills are swallowed annually – we have to armour young people as well as we can against the risks they will run. An attitude of frightened avoidance is not the way to deal with the reality of drugs. What young people need is relaxed, wise information about the use and abuse of drugs, not a panic silence or vague admonishments.

A clear pointer that comes from Alice's diary – and is confirmed from other sources – is that lack of personal confidence, and poor social assurance, make young people vulnerable to drugs. Drugs got their grip on Alice because they made her feel 'wonderful', whereas she usually felt inferior and unwanted.

Often parents are tempted to 'push' a socially awkward child. But pressure and criticism can only increase feelings of personal inadequacy. The adolescent of poor social ability – a handicap that may be linked with physical unattractiveness, real or imagined – needs constant, patient encouragement and a gentle weaning from his, or her, isolation.

If an adolescent does get caught up in the drug scene, what happens next depends very much on two things.

One is the moral climate of the home. Too slack or too prim is equally undesirable. Conventional and 'respectable' attitudes are the antithesis of the tolerant, life-affirming attitudes characteristic of the drug set. Alice found it as hard to share her drug problem with her parents as if she had contracted gonorrhoea or been caught shop-lifting. At the very time when Alice *most* needed the support and sympathy of her parents, she could not bring her problems to them because she felt so desperately that she had let their values down. Once the truth was out, the parents were kind and loving, but they were not 'open' enough to encourage confidence in the vital early stages. A moralizing attitude is, today, fatal to good relationships with adolescents.

The second vital factor is good communications between child and parents, *from an early age.* This, in turn, depends upon a happy acceptance of the individuality of the child. A child who feels loved, *and accepted in his own right,* will share his thoughts, feelings and set-backs with his parents – especially, as a rule, with his mother – all the way up through the years. In such a case, the problems of adolescence will usually be shared, in their turn. But when such close, sympathetic, reassuring communication has not been attained prior to adolescence, parents may be deceived by the front adolescents put on to cover up their shaky self-esteem, and

may think all is well when it certainly is not. Adolescents are so good at covering up that parents and
teachers may remain totally unaware of acute stress.

The most disturbing part of this diary is the dreadful
isolation in which Alice found herself when she was trying
to give up drugs. This involved breaking the bond that
drug-users form with one another. Meanwhile she was, for
some time, rejected by the 'straight' ones. So her search to
become accepted as a person, and the means she chanced
on to attain this – the drug boost – eventually led to her
becoming completely isolated. The conflict, at this stage,
must have been extremely painful. Alice wanted so much
to be independent of drugs, and to vindicate herself in the
eyes of her parents, but this left her without friends while
the drug world – its lift, its warmth, its companionship –
was still close and available.

Alice longed to escape, but at what sort of cost? The
guilt was still there – particularly the guilt of having
been a pusher. The kindness of her parents and eventually of her 'straight' friends only seemed to accentuate
this. Meanwhile the drug group was bitterly attacking
her for 'shopping' one of their members – the unforgiv-
able crime in drug circles. She was now quite alone. She
had started her adolescence with a gnawing sense of
inadequacy. Following the drug encounter, with all its
varied ramifications, she felt even less adequate and,

now, profoundly guilty. It seemed to her that she had betrayed everybody. At that stage, she lost heart, gave up her diary – the *only* friend she could *really* talk to, which had now become a kind of masquerade, a way of reassuring herself, not of expressing herself – and within three weeks was dead, presumably from an overdose.

It is not easy to be parents of adolescents. Adolescents are often brash, demanding, variable, irritating. But they do so much need us at their side as friends and guides in their struggle to grow up. Without being certain that we really value them as persons, it is hard for them to keep their self-respect intact, and without self-respect the struggle for identity can become an unsupportable task. The 'other world' of drugs then becomes highly alluring. Alice's diary, properly understood, can help us to see a little more clearly what adolescents need from us – above all our humanity, our appreciation, our encouragement and our understanding.

James Hemming

The Backstory

Read the fascinating story of this mysterious
book's first publication

Who's Who in *Go Ask Alice*?

Narrator: Is our narrator's name Alice? It never expressly says so in this book. Through the unnamed narrator's diary entries we see the progression of a young girl through the world of drugs, beginning with the colourful highs of hallucinogens and ending with the murky, dangerous world of hardcore drug-taking. She is fifteen at the start of the story.

Roger: the boy the narrator fancies at the beginning of the story. Later on Roger asks the narrator out and kisses her. Roger soon goes away to military school but the pair keep in touch via letter.

Mom and Daddy: the narrator's parents. It is Daddy's new job as a professor at a university that takes the family away to a new town.

Tim and Alexandria: the narrator's little brother and sister.

Gran and Gramps: the narrator's grandparents.

Gerta: the first friend the narrator makes at her new school.

Beth: a Jewish girl the narrator befriends at her new school and who becomes her first good friend there.

Jill Peters: an acquaintance our narrator bumps into whilst spending the summer with her grandparents. She invites her to a party where some of the drinks are spiked with LSD and the narrator unknowingly drinks one.

Bill Thompson: a friend of Jill. Bill introduces the narrator to torpedoes and speed in a single weekend. The next time they go to a party together Bill and the narrator have sex whilst on LSD.

Doctor Langley: the doctor who prescribes the narrator sleeping pills and then tranquilisers.

Chris: a girl that the narrator meets in a boutique clothes shop. The narrator tries pot for the first time with Chris. Eventually the girls run away together to San Francisco.

Richie: introduced by Chris, the narrator and Richie start going out, though Richie is not all he seems.

Shelia: the tall, glamorous owner of the boutique where Chris gets a job in San Francisco.

VINTAGE CLASSICS

Mario Mellani: the owner of the jewellery shop where the narrator works in San Francisco.

Doris: an abused fourteen-year-old girl the narrator meets in Oregon.

Jan: a girl at school who struggles with drug addiction and who starts to threaten the narrator.

Joel Reems: a student the narrator meets at the university library whilst studying.

Mr and Mrs Larsen: neighbours of the narrator's family.

Babbie: a thirteen-year-old girl the narrator meets in the Youth Center. She has been working as a 'baby prostitute' and is just one of the children at the centre with a shocking story.

Fawn: a 'straight' kid the narrator meets after she is let out of the Youth Center.

The history of *Go Ask Alice*

Go Ask Alice is based on the actual diary of a
fifteen-year-old drug user.

It is not a definitive statement on the middle-
class, teenage drug world. It does not offer any
solutions.

It is, however, a highly personal and specific
chronicle. As such, we hope it will provide
insights into the increasingly complicated world
in which we live.

Names, dates, places and certain events have
been changed in accordance with the wishes of
those concerned.

The Editors

Go Ask Alice has a long and controversial history. Above is
the statement that has always been printed on the first
page of the book. First published in 1971 in the USA, it was
originally presented as the true diary of a teenage girl who
inadvertently falls into and becomes seduced by the world
of drugs. Over the decades, however, rumours that the
'diary' was in fact a work of fiction have circulated, with
various theories put forward as to who the author could
have been.

Despite the controversy, the book has been an enormous bestseller ever since it was first published. In the early 1970s demand for the book was huge. Libraries reported having difficulty obtaining and keeping enough copies. The number of teenagers who read the diary also most likely far outstrips the number of books sold, as copies were often passed between friends and borrowed from libraries. A high-profile American TV film adaptation of the book, screened in 1973, further added to the book's success.

Accusations that the book is a literary hoax – not a diary but a work of fiction – have kept it in the public eye in more recent decades. But whether you read the book as a true account, or as a novel, its anti-drugs message is very powerful. Today it has sold more than 5 million copies worldwide and has been translated into many different languages.

Censorship

Some adults feel that *Go Ask Alice* glamorises drug use, rather than discourages it. For that reason it has been one of the most banned books in the US over the years. Many libraries refused to display the book on the shelves and would only lend it to people who specifically requested it.

Today, many readers find the references to homosexuality offensive. These sorts of views were much more commonly held at the time that the book was written but are clearly dated and shocking to a modern reader.

The title

There has been much speculation about the title of *Go Ask Alice*. Who is Alice? Is it the name of the narrator? Some readers have suggested it is a reference to *Alice's Adventures in Wonderland* – a book full of weird, wonderful images.

Lots of people recognise the title from a famous 1967 Jefferson Airplane song 'White Rabbit' about Lewis Carroll's *Alice's Adventures in Wonderland*, taking it as a metaphor for hallucinogenic drug experience.

Drugs – some information

There are a lot of drugs mentioned in *Go Ask Alice* and many of the street names used by our narrator are no longer in use. Here is some information about the drugs referenced in the book. Many of the drugs listed below are controlled substances in most countries around the world, meaning that although some have medicinal uses it is illegal to buy, sell or ingest them recreationally.

Barbs: Barbiturates are drugs that have a wide range of uses including general anaesthesia and euthanising animals. They make you feel relaxed. They can be psychologically and physically addictive.

Grass: A slang word for cannabis, a plant that can be smoked or eaten. Its effects range from feeling lazy to getting the giggles.

Marijuana: Another word for cannabis.

Pot: Another slang word for cannabis common in the 60s and 70s.

Amphetamines: A family of drugs that cause increased alertness and faster reaction times. Medicinally they are used to treat ADHD and obesity.

Speed: A type of amphetamine that makes people feel energised and alert, followed by a long, slow come-down.

Dexie: Short for dextroamphetamine, another type of amphetamine. During the Second World War the drug was used by military air forces to keep pilots alert and to prevent them feeling fatigue. This might be the origin of the slang name for the drug, 'co-pilots'.

LSD: LSD stands for lysergic acid diethylamide. It is a psychedelic drug that is mainly used recreationally. It can give users hallucinations both good and bad. It is not addictive but overuse can lead to paranoia and delusions.

Acid: Another name for LSD.

Heroin: Heroin was first made in 1874 from morphine, a natural product of the opium poppy. Its effects include euphoria and pain relief. It is highly physically addictive and is most often injected directly into a vein, though it can also be smoked or snorted.

Smack: A slang name for heroin.

Paregoric: The principal active ingredient in paregoric is powdered opium. It was available over the counter in the US until 1970. It can be used to treat diarrhoea.

Uppers and downers: A casual way of distinguishing between stimulants and depressants.

Glue: Sniffing glue is not illegal but can be fatal. Some glues and aerosols give off toxic gases that can make you feel dizzy and drunk when sniffed.

The setting for *Go Ask Alice*

Go Ask Alice is set during the late sixties. The story starts during the summer of 1968, a time of immense social upheaval throughout the USA.

The US at that time was experiencing a growing anti-Vietnam War sentiment as well as a civil rights movement that sought racial equality. We see this on page 144 when the narrator's father takes her to an anti-war rally at the university.

The sixties also saw a sexual revolution. The Pill was first available in the USA in 1960. Casual sex became much more socially acceptable, especially within the counter-culture movement. Beginning in San Francisco in the mid-60s, a new culture of 'free love' emerged, with thousands of young people enjoying a more liberated attitude to sex and calling themselves 'hippies'.

The sixties also gave birth to a distinctive youth culture and style, including long hair for boys and girls, short skirts, extravagant prints and generally a more unconventional attitude to appearance. Young people at that time were the first generation not to look like younger versions of their parents. The idea of a teenager as a distinct phase of life was being born.

Hand in hand with the counter-culture movement, prescription and recreational drug use was dramatically on the rise. There were reportedly 50,000 drug-related deaths in the US in 1968. We see the shockingly liberal use of prescription drugs in the story when Doctor Langley prescribes the narrator sleeping pills and then tranquilisers before understanding the root cause of her worries.

What should I read now?

Go Ask Alice was the YA phenomenon of its day. If you enjoyed it you might like some of these other books.

Confessions of an English Opium-Eater by Thomas De Quincy: Probably the first literary memoir by a drug addict, first published in 1821.

Fear and Loathing in Las Vegas by Hunter S. Thompson: Based on two trips the author took to Las Vegas with his attorney and friend in 1971. A story of endless drug benders and a meditation on the collapse of the American Dream.

Trainspotting by Irvine Welsh: A cult classic about being a junkie set in Scotland.

Junk by Melvin Burgess: Told from multiple viewpoints, *Junk* is about a group of teenagers in the grip of heroin addiction.